DEFYING
THE PRINCE

Sarah Morgan

First published in Great Britain 2012
by Mills & Boon, an imprint of Harlequin (UK) Limited,
Large Print edition 2012
Harlequin (UK) Limited,
Eton House, 18-24 Paradise Road, Richmond, Surrey TW9 1SR

© Harlequin Books S.A. 2012

Special thanks and acknowledgement are given to Sarah Morgan
for her contribution to *The Santina Crown* series.

ISBN: 978 0 263 23726 9

Harlequin (UK) policy is to use papers that are natural, renewable
and recyclable products and made from wood grown in sustainable
forests. The logging and manufacturing process conform to the
legal environmental regulations of the country of origin.

Printed and bound in Great Britain
by CPI Antony Rowe, Chippenham, Wiltshire

THE SANTINA CROWN

Royalty has never been so scandalous!

STOP PRESS—
Crown Prince in shock marriage

The tabloid headlines…

When HRH Crown Prince Alessandro of Santina proposes to paparazzi favourite Allegra Jackson it promises to be *the* social event of the decade— outrageous headlines guaranteed!

The salacious gossip…

Mills & Boon invites you to rub shoulders with royalty, sheikhs and glamorous socialites. Step into the decadent playground of the world's rich and famous…

THE SANTINA CROWN

THE PRICE OF ROYAL DUTY
Penny Jordan

THE SHEIKH'S HEIR
Sharon Kendrick

THE SCANDALOUS PRINCESS
Kate Hewitt

THE MAN BEHIND THE SCARS
Caitlin Crews

DEFYING THE PRINCE
Sarah Morgan

PRINCESS FROM THE SHADOWS
Maisey Yates

THE GIRL NOBODY WANTED
Lynn Raye Harris

PLAYING THE ROYAL GAME
Carol Marinelli

SARAH MORGAN

USA TODAY bestselling author Sarah Morgan writes lively, sexy stories for both Mills & Boon® Modern™ Romance and Medical™ Romance.

As a child Sarah dreamed of being a writer, and although she took a few interesting detours on the way she is now living that dream. With her writing career she has successfully combined business with pleasure, and she firmly believes that reading romance is one of the most satisfying and fat-free escapist pleasures available. Her stories are unashamedly optimistic, and she is always pleased when she receives letters from readers saying that her books have helped them through hard times.

RT Book Reviews has described her writing as 'action-packed and sexy', and nominated her books for their Reviewer's Choice Awards and their 'Top Pick' slot.

Sarah lives near London with her husband and two children, who innocently provide an endless supply of authentic dialogue. When she isn't writing or reading Sarah enjoys music, movies, and any activity that takes her outdoors.

Readers can find out more about Sarah and her books from her website: www.sarahmorgan.com. She can also be found on Facebook and Twitter.

CHAPTER ONE

SHE was a shameless exhibitionist.

Prince Matteo, second in line to the throne of Santina and hardened cynic, watched in grim-faced silence as a girl with a rippling mane of streaky blonde hair flirted outrageously with the lead singer of the local band which had been carefully vetted and approved as 'suitable' entertainment by palace officials.

This was a royal engagement party but apparently she hadn't let the dress code printed clearly on her invitation inhibit her choice of outfit for the evening. Wearing a dress of sparkling scarlet sequins, she stood out like a single slender poppy in a bouquet of white roses. Her appearance was sending out myriad messages to the stunned onlookers. Her towering peep-toed shoe-boots said *naughty*, the daring strapless dress cried *look at me*, her scarlet mouth shouted *take me*.

As her hair slid back to reveal smooth, bare shoulders, Matteo could almost feel the texture against his palms and taste the smoothness of her throat under his lips. Everything about her made him think of strawberries: that endless ripple of long blonde hair with its faint suggestion of pink; those rounded breasts pushing happily against that scarlet sequined dress; and those lips, those lips made him think of ripe, sweet, juicy fruit. Not the cultivated variety that were heaped into bowls for palace garden parties but the small wild strawberries that grew in abundance in the rich soil around his palazzo on the rugged west coast of the island.

Wild.

The word summed her up perfectly.

As he watched, those lips curved into a wickedly sexy smile. An explosion of raw sexual heat burned through his body and the intensity of that reaction shocked him because he considered himself not just discerning when it came to the female sex but impervious to their tricks.

Matteo turned to his older brother. 'I presume from the total lack of social graces, her surname is Jackson and she's going to be another of your dubious relations.'

Alex lifted his glass. 'She's my future sister-in-law. Allegra's half-sister.'

'I thought the idea was to boost the reputation of the monarchy, not destroy it.' Even without confirmation from his brother he would have known that she was yet another member of the notorious Jackson family, most of whom were currently grinding vampy stilettos through centuries of royal protocol. 'Why are you doing this?' *Was it his imagination or was his brother drinking more than usual?*

'I'm in love with her.' Alex's gaze rested on his fiancée, Allegra Jackson, also resplendent in red, although her dress was considerably more restrained than her sister's. 'And she's in love with me.'

'Would she be "in love" with you if you weren't a prince?'

Alex gave a twisted smile. 'Ouch, that's harsh.'

'It's honest.' Matteo didn't apologise. At a young age he'd learned in the most brutal way possible to be suspicious of human nature and the lesson hadn't just been well learned. It had formed him.

Briefly, his gaze met his brother's.

Alex frowned. 'This is different.'

'You're sure?' An unwanted memory uncurled in his subconscious, like a wisp of smoke from a fire long extinguished. Without thinking Matteo glanced down at his left hand, at the less than per-fect alignment of his index finger and the silvery scar that was now no more than a faint line from his wrist to this knuckle. Similar scars crossed his ribs and the upper part of his back. His chest tightened and, just for a moment, he was back on the ground with his face pressed into the dirt, feeling the trickle of his own blood on the back of his neck. Right there, right then, choking on his mistakes, almost dying of them, he'd realised that his relationships would never be like other people's. Did love even exist? He had no idea. He just knew it didn't exist for him. And he doubted it existed for his brother. 'I've yet to meet a woman who can separate the man from the title.'

'And you've met plenty.' Alex gave a faint smile. 'You mock the Jackson reputation but your own isn't exactly squeaky clean. Fast women, fast cars, fast jets.'

'Not any more.'

'Last time I looked you were still driving a sports car and escorting the delightful Katarina.'

'I was talking about the jets.' He missed it, he realised, more than he would have anticipated given the years that had passed. 'And we were talking about your engagement—'

'No, *you* were delivering dire warnings. Have you *ever* trusted a woman?'

Just the once. 'Do I look like a fool?'

He knew that everyone he met had an agenda. He knew that those who spoke to him, approached him, flirted with him, all of them were interested in what he was and what he could do for them, not who he was. As a result, he trusted no one. And he especially didn't trust the Jackson swaying seductively on the stage. She looked as if she'd just dragged herself from a wild night in someone's bed and hadn't even bothered to brush her hair. Her raw sex appeal jarred in the atmosphere of rigid restraint and Matteo wondered if he was the only person in the room with a sick feeling of foreboding. Yes, the king wanted his eldest son living in Santina and taking up his responsibilities as Crown Prince, but did he want it so badly he was prepared to sanction a liaison with a family like the Jacksons? On the surface the public was in love with the idea of a prince marrying a commoner, but how much would they love it when the whole thing came crashing down?

He wasn't even aware of the tension in his shoulders until he felt the dull ache spread through his muscles.

This felt so wrong.

Experience told him that the girl on the stage was the worst kind of opportunist. 'She is loud and attention seeking. She looks like a ripe plum that's going to burst out of its skin at any minute.' He switched from strawberries to plums because he disliked plums. It was a more comfortable analogy.

'But very sexy.'

It seemed like an odd comment from a man at his own engagement party and Matteo would have said more but at that moment he saw a group of Jacksons gathered round a priceless portrait and winced as he heard the oohs and aahs.

'They're trying to guess the price of the Holbein.'

As one of them commented in a loud voice that the colours were a bit dull, he closed his eyes briefly, wondering whether there was any way of stopping this before it exploded. 'They don't know Michelangelo from Michael Jackson. Is she really going to be your mother-in-law?' Watching Chantelle Jackson peer at a priceless vase, Matteo shook his head in disbelief. 'Any moment now she is going to drop it into her bag. And no doubt it will be for sale on the internet on Monday.' Suddenly he wished he had a closer relationship with Alex. 'You were supposed to be marrying Anna. What happened?'

'I fell in love.'

Something about that bland response didn't ring true and Matteo wondered whether this engagement was an act of rebellion on Alex's part. 'Perhaps you should take more time?'

'I know exactly what I'm doing.' He paused. 'And Chantelle won't be my mother-in-law. She is Allegra's stepmother.'

It seemed like an odd comment. Matteo was about to ask a few probing questions when he saw that the strawberry girl was now centre stage.

And suddenly those knowing eyes were fixed on him as she started singing a song she dedicated to her sister, a song about getting your guy, which was all too appropriate, Matteo thought.

In the world of social climbing his brother had to be the equivalent of Mount Everest.

No wonder the Jacksons were celebrating.

As she leaned forward and sang cheekily into the microphone he saw movement out of the corner of his eye as Bobby Jackson, an ex-footballer whose colourful and varied love life was catalogued by the tabloids, tried to remove his daughter from the limelight.

Matteo watched with mixed feelings.

It was definitely time someone prised her away from the microphone, but the fact that it was the flamboyant, scandal-ridden Bobby simply magnified the transgression.

'Come on, love.' Bobby Jackson made a clumsy grab for his daughter's arm but she shrugged him off and he almost lost his balance. 'Give the microphone back, there's a good girl.' His face was the colour of a Santina sunset. The deep hue could have been the result of intense embarrassment but Matteo suspected it was more likely to have been caused by an overindulgence of the very best champagne. Bobby Jackson was too thick-skinned to suffer from embarrassment. Matteo knew he'd dragged himself up from nothing and was determined that his family should do the same, although apparently that ambition didn't stretch to encouraging his daughter to sing.

Matteo glanced at his own father and saw that the king's features were as rigid and inflexible as one of Michelangelo's statues.

'Izzy!' Bobby made another abortive grab for his daughter. 'Not now. Best behaviour and all that.'

Izzy.

Of course.

Matteo realised where he'd seen her before. He recognised her now as the five-minute wonder who had exploded onto the manufactured pop scene after appearing on a reality TV singing show. Izzy Jackson. Hadn't she hit the headlines for wearing a bikini on stage? Basically for doing everything but singing. Presumably she had a voice like a crow with a throat infection, like most of the wannabes that warbled and croaked their way onto people's TV screens, which was why he remembered nothing about her singing.

Even her own family didn't want her to sing in public, he thought, watching as her father tried to drag her from the stage.

It was like pulling a mule. She dug her legs in and stood, chin raised, eyes flashing as she carried on belting out the tune.

It was clear that she thought this was her opportunity to shine and she wasn't going to relinquish it easily, a fact that raised Matteo's radar for trouble to full alert status.

'Maybe we should turn this whole farce into a reality TV show,' he drawled to his brother. *'Celebrity Love Palace? I'm a Prince, Get Me Out of Here?'*

'Do me a favour? Get *her* out of here. The focus

of attention *has* to be on my engagement.' Alex spoke with an urgency that rang alarm bells in Matteo's brain.

'Are you going to tell me why?'

'Just do it, Matt. Please.'

Without further question Matteo handed his champagne to a passing footman.

'You owe me. And I *will* be calling in the favour.'

With that he strode across the room to separate trouble from the microphone.

'He's the only one for yooooou...' sang Izzy in her rich alto voice, pleased with herself for hitting a fiendishly difficult note right at the top of her range and furious when her father tried to prise her away from the microphone.

Wasn't he the one who was always telling her that it was up to her to make the most of opportunities? Well, this was a massive opportunity. She'd planned it carefully. Her Goal of the Day was to sing the song she'd written to the prince. Not the smiling, charming heir to the throne that her sister had snagged, but his brother, Matteo Santina, the Dark Prince, otherwise known to a fascinated public as Moody Matteo because he was so deadly serious. Deadly serious and deadly sexy, Izzy thought dreamily. He was tall, dark, gorgeous and very, very rich. But she wasn't interested in any of those attributes. She wasn't interested in his spectacular bone structure or his royal heritage. Nor did she care about his hard athletic body or his reputed skills as a pilot. And although the romantic side of her was mildly jealous of her sister's whirlwind romance, she wasn't the least interested in the whole marry-a-prince fantasy. No, there was just one thing she cared about and that was the extent of his influence—in particular, his role as president of the Prince's Fund. In that role he had overall responsibility for the famous Rock 'n' Royal concert, a globally televised live fundraising event that was only weeks away.

Singing at that concert would be all her dreams rolled into one. It would kick-start her dead career.

Which was why today's goal was to make sure he heard her.

Shaking off her father, she increased the volume, but the prince was now in conversation with his brother, the heir to the throne and her sister's fiancé.

Izzy felt a frantic moment of desperation followed by a sharp thud of disappointment. She'd been so sure that this would be her big moment.

She'd glugged down the champagne to give herself the courage to take over the stage. She'd imagined heads turning and jaws dropping as people heard her voice. She'd imagined her whole life changing in an instant. Hard work and perseverance was going to *finally* pay off.

Heads *were* turning. Jaws *were* dropping. But Izzy hadn't drunk so much champagne that she didn't realise her being the centre of attention had nothing to do with her voice.

They were looking at her because she'd made a fool of herself. Again.

They were mocking her.

So, in fact, her life hadn't changed at all because, as usual, she was on the receiving end of ridicule. Each time she dragged herself back onto her feet she was knocked over again, and each time she emerged just a little more bruised and battered.

The confidence-boosting buzz from the champagne was morphing into a horrid spinning feeling.

Aware of the unsmiling disapproval on the aristocratic faces around her, she decided that Allegra had to be *seriously* in love if she was prepared to put up with this. As far as Izzy could see, marrying a prince promised about as interesting a future as being stuffed and put in a glass case in a museum for everyone to stare at. What was that called? Taxi-something or other. And she was so *hungry*, and she could never think properly when she was hungry. Why on earth weren't they serving proper food? She would have killed for a bacon roll and all they'd given her since she'd arrived was champagne, champagne and more champagne.

The royals certainly knew how to drink. Unfortunately they didn't seem to eat which probably explained why they were all so thin. And why she'd broken her golden rule and drunk too much.

'Just one love—' she hollered happily, beaming at a group of women who were gazing at her in disapproval and ignoring her father's less than subtle attempts to tempt her from the stage.

The fact that even her family didn't listen added a sting to the already sharp pain of humiliation. Weren't families supposed to support you no matter what? She *adored* them but they patted her on the head and patronized her as if she was singing drunk at a karaoke machine rather than giving her all. She *knew* she had a good voice. And even if they didn't like the song and thought she was foolish trying to make a career from what should have been a hobby, they ought to be grateful to her for trying to liven up a totally boring evening.

'Enough!' Her father's loud voice boomed around the ornate room, his East London accent jarring with the cultured tones around him confirming the one thing everyone already knew—that no amount of money could buy class. Izzy already knew that. She knew exactly how people felt about her family. 'Save the singing for when you're in the shower. You're embarrassing yourself, luv.'

No, I'm not, Izzy thought. *I'm embarrassing you.* And the hypocrisy of it stung. She loved her father, but even she knew his behaviour was often questionable. And now they were laughing at *her*, and the sharp sting of their mockery was all the more acute because Izzy had been so desperate for them to take her seriously.

It was partly her fault, she acknowledged miserably. She should never have entered that stupid reality show *Singing Star*. She'd done it because she'd thought that finally someone would hear her voice but the producers had been less interested in the sound she could belt out than in the picture she'd made on the stage and the gimmick factor of having tabloid-favourite Bobby Jackson's daughter on the show. They'd made her do all sorts of dubious things to raise the ratings, none of which had focused on her singing. And she'd been too wrapped up in her own fleeting moment of fame to see the truth.

Until it was too late.

Until she'd become a national joke.

The fame had vanished faster than water down the drain, and with it her reputation. Forever more she was going to be 'that awful girl from *Singing Star.*'

Unable to think about that without squirming, Izzy turned away, closed her eyes and sang, pouring out the notes and losing herself in the music until her concentration was shattered by someone closing a cold, hard handcuff around her wrist.

She was being arrested for crimes against music.

Her eyes flew open in shock and she realised it wasn't a handcuff, but someone's fingers, brutally hard and as cold and unyielding as metal. Her startled gaze collided with unfriendly dark eyes and the sound died in her throat.

It was the prince.

Raw sexual attraction ripped through her because close up he was quite simply the most spectacular man she'd ever met, even more incredible to look at than all the photographs had led her to believe. A television camera might hint at the thickness of those dark lashes and the perfect shape of his mouth but no lens, however powerful, could capture the innate masculinity that set him apart from others.

'Enough.' He spoke through his teeth, his tone so abrupt that even the normally buoyant and resilient Izzy felt herself shrivel.

The Prince and the Pauper, she thought, struggling to keep her balance on her towering platform shoe-boots as he all but yanked her from the stage.

Clearly he had no intention of formally introducing himself—presumably because he didn't see the need. Everyone knew who he was. And he was living up to his formidable reputation, his spectacular features set and severe as he bodily removed her from her position by the musicians.

So that was that then—

Watching her dream of stardom fizzle out and realising that the last glass of champagne she'd downed had pushed her over the edge from tipsy to drunk, Izzy stumbled as she attempted to twist her wrist from his grip. 'Ouch! What are you doing? I was just singing, that's all. Do you mind not gripping so hard? I have a very low pain threshold and don't drag me because these shoes definitely aren't made for walking.' Swamped by the wave of disapproval flowing from the other guests, she was grateful for the anaesthetising effects of the alcohol.

'Off with her head,' she whispered dramatically, smiling sweetly as he sent a black glare in her direction. 'Oops—we are definitely not amused.' Her heart sank.

So much for hoping he might be able to relaunch her stalled singing career.

It was clear from his body language that he wouldn't be likely to give her a job cleaning the toilets at the palace let alone a role in the upcoming concert.

Izzy Jackson wasn't going to feature on his list of headline acts. And she couldn't even blame him because she knew she hadn't sung her best. She'd tried too hard. Forced her voice.

As he towed her across the room he spoke in a low, driven voice intended only for her. 'You are a guest, *not* the entertainment. And you're drunk.' Although it wasn't his first language, he spoke English as fluently as she did but that was where the similarity ended. His aristocratic demeanour had been bred into him and polished by the best education money could buy. His mother was a monarch. Hers was a market stall trader. His accent was cut glass. Hers was shatterproof plastic tableware.

'Actually I'm not drunk.' Izzy was swamped by disappointment that her plans had gone so badly wrong. 'At least, not very. And even if I am then it's your fault for serving buckets of alcohol and no food.' She glanced desperately around for a friendly face and caught sight of her sister, but Allegra wasn't looking at her either, clearly trying to distance herself from Izzy's behaviour. Stung by that betrayal and mortified her surprise song that she'd been working on for weeks had been received with the same enthusiasm as a virus, she momentarily lost her bounce. *What did she have to do to make people listen?*

'All right, you've made your point. I messed up. Let me go, and I promise to be boringly appropriate. I'll stand still and talk about the weather or whatever it is that these people talk about without moving their faces.' Hoping to end it there, she pulled and struggled but he ignored her attempts to free herself and propelled her past an astonished-looking footman, through a door into a panelled anteroom lined with portraits.

'Stop dragging me! I can't walk fast in these heels.'

'Then why wear such ridiculous shoes?'

'I'm small.' Izzy tried desperately to keep her balance. 'If I don't wear heels people just look over the top of my head. I'm trying to make an impression.'

'Congratulations, you succeeded.' His tone left her in no doubt as to what sort of impression she had made.

Rows of his ancestors glared down at her from large gilt frames and Izzy scowled back at their stony faces.

'Why do they all look so miserable? Isn't *anyone* in your family happy? I wish I'd never come.'

'We all share that sentiment.' He sent a single glance towards the uniformed footman and the door was closed. They were alone.

'Another door closes,' Izzy whispered dramatically, and his fingers tightened on her wrist. She could feel the leashed strength and the flow of tension through his hard frame. His superior height meant that she had to tilt her head to look at him and doing so made her head swim.

'Er, do you think you could stop gripping me?' *He smelt good*, she thought absently. *Really good.* 'It's not like I'm going to run off. I can barely walk in these shoes, let alone sprint.'

He released her instantly, the contempt in his eyes adding a few more bruises to her already battered confidence.

Much as she hated to admit it, she found him horribly intimidating.

He was so *sure* of himself. This man had never been beaten to the ground and had to pull himself up again. He positively *throbbed* power and authority and he made her feel as insignificant as a spec of dust. And then there were the other feelings. The feelings she didn't want to think about. Like the dangerous crawl of lust deep in her belly and the burn of heat where the press of his strong fingers had branded her skin.

Rejecting those feelings instantly, Izzy took a step backwards. 'I was just *singing*. I wasn't naked, or using bad language or telling awful jokes. I wanted you to notice me.'

His eyes flared with shock. 'You treated my

brother's engagement party as a way of targeting me? How brazen can you get?'

'Pretty brazen. You don't get anywhere in life by holding yourself back.' Izzy put her weight on one leg to try and relieve the throbbing pain in her feet. 'I know what I want and I go after it.'

'I have had women throw themselves at me at the most inopportune moments but your performance has eclipsed everything that has gone before.'

'Eclipsed in a good way?' The sudden hopeful lift in her spirits was immediately squashed by his condescending glare. 'Obviously *not* in a good way. So you're not interested. Never mind. It's not the first time I've tried and failed. I'll get over it.'

She wondered why he was so angry. It wasn't as if she'd hurt anyone. As he prowled around the room Izzy's eyes followed him in reluctant fascination. The man was a global sex symbol and up close it was all too easy to see why.

'Do you think you could stop moving? I'm feeling a bit weird and watching you is making me dizzy.' Or maybe it wasn't the movement, she thought. Maybe it was the way his undoubtedly super-expensive jacket failed to conceal the power of the body underneath.

'How much have you drunk?' The snap of his tone should have shredded the tension but instead it seemed to intensify the lethal, suffocating heat.

Finding it difficult to breathe, Izzy gripped the back of the chair tightly. 'I haven't drunk enough to get me through a night like this, believe me. And it's not my fault that those people in uniform—'

'They're called footmen—'

'—yes, them—they kept filling up my glass and I didn't like to say no and offend anyone.' The words tumbled out of her like water in a fast-flowing stream. 'And anyway, I was thirsty because it's hot in there but there was no food to mop up the alcohol, just those tiny canapé things that get stuck in your teeth and don't fill you up. *And*, might I remind you, this is supposed to be a party. I was trying to lighten the atmosphere. It's like a funeral in there, not an engagement. If this is the life my sister can expect when she marries your brother then I feel sorry for her.' She stopped, distracted by a masculine face so impossibly handsome that it almost hurt to look at him.

Despite his almost unnatural stillness, she knew he was angry. She could *feel* the anger in him beneath that sophisticated, polished veneer. Izzy was wondering whether it would make him even angrier if she removed her shoes before they cut off her blood supply when those dark eyes burned into hers.

'You planned this whole thing, didn't you?'

'Yes, I did.' Hadn't she just told him that? 'Every day I set a goal. It helps me stay focused. Today you were my goal.'

'*Cristo*. You admit it?'

'Of course.' *What was wrong with having goals?* 'I confess to the crime, Your Honour.' She gave a little salute and almost lost her balance.

'Is everything a joke to you?'

'I try and laugh at life when I can.' And her career was definitely a joke, she thought gloomily. A big, fat joke.

'You are loud and indiscreet. If you're going to be linked with our family you need to learn to filter what you say.'

Izzy thought about all the times people had said one thing to her and meant another.

Dress like this and you'll be a star, Izzy.

I love you, Izzy.

Her insides lurched. She wasn't going to think about that now. Or later. 'By "filter," you mean lie? You want me to be like those women out there with frozen smiles and non-existent expressions who don't actually say anything they mean? Sorry, but that's just not me.'

'I'm sorry too. The fact that your sister is marrying the future king makes you of interest to the public.'

'Really?' Izzy brightened at the prospect that someone might actually be interested in her. 'Now that's what I call a happy ending.'

Disapproval throbbed from every inch of his powerful frame. 'If this marriage has a chance of being accepted by the public then you will need to be kept out of the public eye. We cannot afford the negative publicity. The focus needs to be on Alex and Allegra. And if your sister is marrying the future king you need to learn how to behave. And how to dress.' That gaze skimmed her body and she felt as if she'd been singed by the flame of a blowtorch.

Either he was giving off mixed messages or her emotional radar was jammed. There was disapproval there, yes, but there was also something else. A dangerous undercurrent that she couldn't read properly.

'It's not my dress that's wrong, it's your party. No one in this place knows how to laugh, dance or have a good time. Those chandeliers are all very well but you could have done with a few disco balls to liven things up.'

'This is a royal palace, not a nightclub. Your behaviour should reflect that.'

'So I'm supposed to curtsey?' Her flippant tone was met with derision.

'Yes.' His voice was silky smooth, his manner dangerously cool and his temper ruthlessly controlled. Everything about him was restrained. 'And the correct mode of address is "Your Royal Highness."'

She barely heard him. Her mind had ripped itself free of her control and her thoughts flew free as her eyes drifted to the strong lines of his jaw and from there to the sensual shape of his mouth. Something about that mouth told her that he'd know exactly how to kiss a woman. Heat flashed through her and suddenly all she could think of was sex, which shocked her because after her own disastrous experience and the permanent example of her parents' highly dysfunctional marriage, getting involved with a man definitely wasn't one of her goals.

For a moment they just stared at each other and

then he frowned. 'After the first time you can call me "Sir."'

'The first time'?' Her heart was hammering and her mouth was so dry that she could barely form the words. 'There's never going to be a "first time." I wouldn't sleep with you if I was desperate which, by the way, I absolutely am not. I'm not like that. I'm a really romantic person.'

Exasperation flickered across his face. '*Were* desperate,' he breathed. 'The correct grammar is "were" not "was." You use the past subjunctive when stating conditions that are contrary to fact. And I was talking about the correct manner of address the first time you meet me. Nothing else.'

Izzy, who had never heard of the subjunctive and whose only interest in English was its use in writing song lyrics, felt her face burn. 'Right. Well, it's excellent to have that cleared up so early in a relationship.' Utterly mortified by the misunderstanding, which she could see now was entirely her doing and had been caused by the fact that she'd been thinking about sex with him, she ploughed on. 'Do I seriously have to call you "Sir"? It's just that the only person I ever called "Sir" is my old headmaster and thinking about him brings back a lot of memories I usually try and forget.'

'The man has my deepest sympathy. Teaching you must have been a challenge to exceed all others.' He stood directly in front of the largest painting in the room and Izzy saw the similarities immediately. The same cropped black hair. The same dark, dangerous looks. *The same aristocratic lineage.*

No wonder he was arrogant, she thought numbly. His breeding went back centuries whereas she was just a mongrel. The product of two people who had each wanted something from the other.

To make herself feel better she wanted to dismiss him but there was no ignoring the width and power of those shoulders. She didn't want to find him attractive, but what woman wouldn't? Her insides squirmed and a slow, dangerous heat spread through her pelvis.

It had to be the champagne, she thought. It was intensifying everything she felt. 'Doesn't the formality drive you mad? No one actually smiles or moves their faces. It's like being in a room of those stone statue things we passed on the way in.'

'Those priceless *marble* statues date back to the fifteenth century.'

'That's a long time to keep your face in one position. And I'm not surprised they're priceless. Who the hell would want to pay money to have something that miserable staring at you? Sir.' She added it as an afterthought, seriously worried by how fast the room was spinning. 'I would curtsey but honestly these shoes are completely killing me so right now I'm trying not to move. If you were a girl, you'd understand.'

He growled deep in his throat. 'You are the most frivolous, pointless woman I've ever met. Your behaviour is appalling and the damage that someone like you could do to the reputation of my family is monumental.'

Izzy, who had been called many things in her life but never 'pointless,' was deeply hurt but at the same time oddly grateful because surely she could never truly fall for a man who was so horribly insulting? 'I happen to think it's *your* behaviour that's appalling. Why is it good behaviour to make someone feel small and inferior? You think you're better than me, but if someone comes into my house I smile at them and make them feel welcome whereas you look down on everyone. I've had more impressive hospitality in a burger bar. You may be a prince and actually far too sexy for your own good, but you don't know anything about manners.' Lifting her nose in the air she was about to say something else when the door opened and a white-faced member of the palace staff stood there.

'The microphone, Your Royal Highness,' he said in a strangled voice, addressing himself to the stony-faced prince. 'It's still switched on. Everything you're saying can be heard in the ball-room. On high volume.'

CHAPTER TWO

APPALLED by the realisation that his family and guests had overheard their exchange, Matteo froze. He, who prided himself on his self-control, had lost it. Publicly.

As he re-ran the conversation in his head, he wanted to groan.

Sex...

How had the conversation turned to sex?

He couldn't remember when he'd last allowed his emotions to dictate his behaviour but from the moment he'd laid eyes on those strawberry-red lips and that enticing dress he'd felt his grip on control slipping. He prided himself on his focus. He'd flown jets faster than the speed of sound, negotiated sensitive deals with foreign governments, raised millions for charity and yet he hadn't managed to control the behaviour of one aggravating young woman.

The best he could hope for now was damage limitation.

With an authoritative nod he dismissed the palace footman and pointedly removed the microphone from Izzy's hand.

This time she didn't resist and Matteo switched it off, his mouth tightening as he reflected on the awkwardness of their current situation. Having finally secured their privacy he looked at her, expecting to see a similar degree of mortification reflected in those over-made-up eyes, but Izzy Jackson hadn't finished surprising him.

Instead of shrinking with horror at her public exposure, she gave a gurgle of laughter.

Infuriated by that entirely inappropriate response, Matteo's eyes narrowed dangerously. 'This is *not* funny.'

'No, it isn't.' Clearly aware that she wasn't supposed to be laughing, she pressed her lips together but still the sound escaped, so she lifted first one hand and then the other and covered her mouth. But that didn't work either because her eyes swam with tears of laughter, and in the end she gave up the fight and allowed it to escape. Doubling over, she laughed and laughed, apparently highly amused by an incident that had left him cold with horror. And she didn't just laugh with her mouth she laughed with her whole body.

'Sorry. I'm really sorry—you're right, of course, it's absolutely *not* funny—' But she was laughing so hard she could barely speak and neither could Matteo because his eyes were on the seams of her dress which were severely threatened by the unaccustomed strain being placed on them. Her body was lush and ripe and dangerously close to revealing itself.

As if to confirm his fears a single red sequin pinged onto the floor and his loins tightened. The white heat of sexual desire threatened to burn him up and the fact that she was the last woman in the world he would have wanted to feel anything for just made his response all the more exasperating.

Struggling for control, she wiped her eyes with her palm. 'You have to see the funny side. I expect you'll be taking orders for a Quarter Pounder with cheese any minute. With extra fries.'

Matteo somehow held his temper in check, his unfavourable impression of her deepening with each passing second. Any dignified woman would be appalled by what had happened. Not Izzy Jackson. She didn't even bother trying to hide how funny she found the whole episode. In fact she made laughter a physical workout, apparently unaware that leaning forward gave him a prime view of her cleavage. 'You are a one-woman di-saster zone.' But he noticed that his icy censorship appeared to have no impact on her mood.

'I know. I'm sorry.' But she wasn't sorry enough to stop laughing. 'Look on the bright side—it could have been worse. What if we'd sneaked in here to have hot sex and we'd left the microphone switched on? What if you'd grabbed me and said "Izzy, I want you"?' She delivered that dramatic statement complete with hand gestures which rocked her off balance and she swayed into him. 'Oops.'

With a soft curse he closed his hands around her arms and steadied her. He expected her to im-mediately regain her balance and pull away but instead she plopped her head against his chest.

'It's nice to rest for a moment. I wish I hadn't drunk that champagne.'

Her hair smelt of wild flowers and reminded him of the summers he'd spent at the palazzo when he was a child. The memory almost suf-focated him. 'I wish you hadn't drunk it either.' Her arms were bare and her skin was smooth and soft under his fingers. He needed to let her go. Right now.

But if he let her go, she'd fall over.

As if confirming that, she nestled closer. 'I really *am* sorry. I totally and utterly messed up and you deserve to feel very, very cross. But it would be great if you could be cross quietly because I don't feel too good, Your Highness—Sir.'

'You don't deserve to feel good after what you just did.' But there was something about that apology and the way her slim fingers clutched the front of his shirt that touched him and the feeling unsettled him even more than the raw stab of lust because he always remained emotionally detached in his dealings with women. Especially women blatant enough to admit their 'goal' was to marry a prince. 'You're a disaster, Izzy Jackson.'

'I know.' Her voice was muffled against his chest. 'The crazy thing is I don't mean to be a disaster. I start every day with a goal.'

'So you keep telling me.' He tried to unpeel her fingers but her grip tightened.

'I just wanted to impress you.'

'Did you seriously expect your plan to work?' Even the roughness of his voice didn't tempt her to move.

'I hoped you'd take one look at me and just think *wow*. But I think I might have chosen the wrong dress. I didn't get my image right. I need to try again.'

Matteo inhaled deeply. 'Please do *not*. Please give up that goal right now.'

'I *never* give up. I just wish I could put the clock back and do it all again.'

He contemplated telling her that he wouldn't have been interested no matter what she was wearing but the feel of her snuggling closer drove the blood from his brain to a different part of his anatomy.

'Hasn't that ever happened to you?' Her words were slightly slurred. 'Haven't you ever wished you could put the clock back?'

Everyone was scrupulously careful in the way they dealt with him. People tiptoed around him. Men were universally respectful. Women fawned, flattered and flirted. They certainly didn't ask him intimate questions about his thoughts and feelings.

Maybe he was finally getting his comeuppance, Matteo thought. He'd occasionally wished that there was one person in his life who would behave naturally around him, but now that he was faced with the reality he was fast rethinking the perceived benefits. 'Miss Jackson—' his attempt

at formality seemed ridiculous given the circumstances '—Izzy.'

'What?' Reluctantly she lifted her head and
huge eyes heavily outlined in kohl stared up at
him. Sky-blue eyes were fringed by long, thick
eyelashes that surely had to be false.

The scent of her perfume curled itself round
his senses and for a moment his brain refused to
work. She smelt of a summer's day and suddenly
he could see her naked and lush lying in a carpet of bluebells, all that strawberry hair tangled
around her flushed cheeks.

'I truly didn't mean to ruin the party.' Her words
were slightly slurred. 'Are you very, very angry?
Are you going to lock me in the dungeon and
throw away the key?'

Matteo had never found it so hard to concentrate. 'Right now I can't decide whether to shake
you or throw a bucket of cold water over you.'

She pulled a face. 'That doesn't sound nice. For
me or your carpet. Can't you think of something
else to do with me?'

*Crush his mouth to hers and kiss her until they
were both crazy with it?*

*Strip off that outrageous dress and find out if
the rest of her was as soft as her arms?*

His gaze dropped from hazy blue eyes to the perfect curve of her soft, pink lips.

His mouth had moved dangerously close to hers when the door opened.

Matteo released her instantly, but not before he'd seen the surprise in her eyes—surprise he was fairly sure was mirrored by his own expression.

Fury mingling with exasperation, he turned.

His brother's fiancée, Allegra, stood there, her face pale.

Struggling to balance without Matteo holding her, Izzy took a wobbly step backwards, her expression concerned. 'Ally, are you all right?'

'Izzy, how *could* you?' Allegra kept her voice low but if anything that show of restraint intensified the emotion behind her words. 'What did you think you were doing?'

Matteo was asking himself the same question. *What had he been doing?*

Half a minute later and he would have done something both parties would have lived to regret.

Relieved to have been rescued from a course of action that was not only uncharacteristic but would have ended badly, Matteo watched as a shocked flush spread over Izzy's rounded cheeks.

'I was going to sing you a song.' Her tone was defensive and hurt. 'It was something that I—'

'I wasn't talking about the song, although that was embarrassing enough because normal people don't just walk up to someone and grab the microphone. I'm talking about the way you spoke to His Royal Highness.' Allegra's mortified gaze slid to Matteo and she sank into a respectful curtsey. 'I *beg* your pardon, Sir. My sister isn't used to being around royalty.'

'So I gathered.' He tried to ignore the thought that it was precisely her freshness and lack of stilted conversation that made Allegra's sister so dangerously attractive.

Izzy's heavily made-up features were stiff. 'Don't apologise for me,' she said flatly. 'If there's any apologising to do, I'll do it myself.'

'If?' Allegra breathed deeply. 'Of course you should apologise. In fact, if the story in the press tomorrow is about you then you'd probably better make a public apology.'

Matteo watched as Izzy wrapped her arms around herself in a protective gesture that was too much for the dress and another scarlet sequin sprang loose and landed on the priceless Aubusson carpet.

'They say whatever they like, regardless of whether it's true. I don't care. And normally you don't care either.'

'Well, I care now! It will be another bad story about the Jacksons. It's always awful but this time it's doubly embarrassing because you've dragged the royal family into it. This engagement party was supposed to introduce the Jackson family to the people of Santina. It was *supposed* to be about Alex and me. The headlines were supposed to be *Prince in Love* but now they're more likely to be *Hospitality Better at Burger Bar.*' Allegra threw a mortified look of apology to Matteo before turning back to her sister. The girl stood rigid as a flagpole.

'I was just singing. Not the greatest crime known to mankind.'

'They *had* a singer! And you pushed him out of the way because you just had to be the one in the limelight. You need to stop this stupid singing obsession and get a proper job!'

'Singing can be a job.'

'Singing is a dream and dreams don't pay the bills.'

The only sound in the wood panelled room was the deep, resonant tick-tock that came from the eighteenth century clock dominating the ornate mantelpiece.

Pale as milk, Izzy picked at her nails. 'Some people turn a dream into their job.'

'How many? How many people manage that? Thousands, *millions*, of people try and only a handful make it. Stop kidding yourself. Look around you. See the competition.'

Her sister's chin lifted. 'It's only over when you give up. And I won't give up.'

'So you're going to throw away your whole life? You're deluded, Izzy. Ruin your own life if you have to, but I beg you, don't ruin mine.'

Izzy looked shattered, like a delicate vase that had been dropped onto concrete. 'It's not my fault that the press follow me around. It's not like I ask them to.'

Her voice sounded strange and Matteo felt a flicker of concern because he'd never seen anyone look quite so fragile. Standing in those towering heels she swayed like a reed in the wind and he instinctively shifted his weight, ready to catch her if she fell.

Was it the drink causing her balance problems or those ridiculous shoes she'd insisted on wearing?

Either way, she was as white as the marble

statue she'd mocked and it was obvious that she was seriously upset.

Matteo took control. 'Leave it with me. I'll sort it out.'

Relief spread over Allegra's face but Izzy's expression shifted from miserable to mutinous.

'I'm not an "it" and I don't need "sorting out." I'm more than capable of sorting myself out, thank you very much! And if what you want is for me to avoid the press then that's what I'll do.'

Remembering the urgency in his brother's voice, Matteo walked Allegra to the door. 'This is your week. The press should be focusing on you and Alex. That's what we all want. If I take your sister back to the hotel, they'll be staking her out, so I'll get her out of here in my car.' And if part of him knew it was madness to put himself in a position where he'd be spending more time in the company of the most disturbing woman he'd met for a long time then he ignored it. He was a man who prided himself on his self-control. He'd exercise it. The priority was to see his brother safely married and fulfilling the role of Crown Prince. 'My palazzo is heavily guarded and the grounds run straight to steep cliffs and a private beach. No press.' He'd made sure of it. The place was like a fortress. 'It's isolated.'

Allegra's face relaxed with relief as she pondered that solution. 'It sounds perfect. It will give Alex and me a chance to…be together.'

'It sounds like hell!' Izzy's face was white as a bride's veil. 'So I'm just going to move in with you? Well, that's cosy. Lucky me. I just know we're going to live happily ever after. It'll be like a perfect fairy tale.'

Matteo ignored her and addressed his remarks to Allegra. 'Go back to Alex.'

'Hello!' Izzy's voice was high-pitched. 'I'm here too, remember?'

'A fact I am unlikely to forget.' The chill in his tone earned him a wounded look from Izzy and a relieved smile from Allegra.

'Thank you so much.'

A sound emerged from Izzy's throat—it might have been protest, but her sister had already gone, closing the door firmly behind her.

Izzy was staring at the closed door, those black-rimmed eyes huge, as if she couldn't quite believe what had just happened. 'I need to talk to her— she's not behaving like herself.…'

Given his own suspicions about the engagement that comment might have been worth exploring further, but Matteo decided that his brother needed to sort out his own problems. The limit of his intervention was going to be removing this girl from the scene.

Knowing that the press wouldn't expect anyone to leave the party early, Matteo pulled his phone out of his pocket. 'We're leaving right now.'

She stood rigid. 'I don't want to spend another minute with you. Why you're the world's most eligible bachelor I have no idea but I certainly don't want to meet anyone else on that list.'

'Next time you make me your "goal" perhaps you'd better carry out a little more in-depth research,' he advised in a silky tone. 'Did you bring a coat?'

'I don't need a coat. I'm *not* going with you.'

'You can come willingly or I can carry you out of here. Your choice.'

'I'm absolutely not going—oh—' She gave an astonished squeak as he scooped her into his arms and carried her towards the door on the opposite side of the room that led to a private exit. 'Ugh. Don't jiggle me around—I get travel sick. Put me down! It will serve you right if you put your back out.'

'You weigh nothing.' And acknowledging that cost him because it made him more aware of the feel of her in his arms, of the softness of her skin and the way her hair brushed against his jaw.

'I'd weigh more if you fed me. I've lost several kilos since I arrived. Why on earth would you want me to come with you? You hate me.'

If only.

He wondered what she'd say if she knew his feelings towards her were far, far more complex than that. She was so black and white, he thought. So extreme about everything. A small, lethal grenade of passion just waiting to explode at the wrong moment. All the more reason to isolate her somewhere she could do no harm.

Ignoring the astonished glances of the staff, Matteo strode down a set of steps and into a private courtyard at the rear of the palace.

He was just congratulating himself on being back in control of the situation when he felt the warmth of her mouth against his neck. Fire flashed through his veins and heated his body.

'*What* are you doing?' His voice was hoarse and he lowered her abruptly to the ground.

'I asked you nicely to put me down—' she looked as unsteady as she sounded '—but you didn't listen to reason so I'm trying alternative tactics. Flattered though I am that you see someone as small and insignificant as me as some sort of monarchy wrecker, I'm afraid I must refuse your kind invitation to stay at your palazzo. Firstly because I have a suspicion that you're not a very nice person. Secondly because if tonight is anything to go by the hospitality probably isn't up to much, and fourthly—'

'Thirdly,' he corrected her smoothly, and she blinked.

'Whatever. I really liked my hotel room. It came with a big fluffy dressing gown. For one week of my life I was going to live in luxury. I was going to have the whole princess lifestyle without the inconvenience of a prince.'

He was now standing a safe distance from her but he could still feel the touch of her mouth against his skin. 'Your hotel is now a no-go zone. You're coming with me and that isn't an invitation, it's a command.'

'I like to make my own choices, thank you very much.'

'Fine. Here are your choices. You can get in the car yourself, or I can put you there. Move.' With a discreet flick of his wrist Matteo unlocked the sports car. 'And don't you dare be sick.'

At any other time she would have danced with excitement at the prospect of being given another chance to impress him, but Izzy was feeling hideous. And it wasn't all down to the champagne she'd drunk.

She couldn't believe the evening had gone so badly wrong. She needed to regroup. To plan. But she didn't feel well enough.

As she slid into the deep leather seat of the super car, a nasty mixture of misery and humiliation sloshed around her brain mingling with a massive dollop of disappointment. When she'd envisaged the end of the evening none of her daydreams had included her being whisked away under the cover of darkness from a discreet private entrance hidden in the depths of the palace grounds.

She felt like a criminal being removed from the scene of the crime. And the fact that it was just the two of them in the car was deeply unsettling.

'You're a prince. I thought you'd have a bullet-proof limo and armed police.'

'I drive myself.' The engine started with a throaty growl and he pressed his foot to the floor.

'I prefer to be responsible for my own security rather than trusting it to other people.'

'That must be quite a job because after half an hour in your company I'm willing to believe that there must be a million women out there just dying to shoot you through the head.' Izzy had the satisfaction of seeing his knuckles whiten on the wheel. 'You're the one who wanted to kidnap me. Your punishment is being stuck with me.' And her punishment? *Her punishment was the dangerous sizzle that made it difficult to breathe.*

He shifted gears with a smooth, expert movement and the car shot forward with a throaty growl. 'Feel free to sulk over my appalling treatment of you. I would welcome the silence.'

'I never sulk.' But deep down she was bitterly disappointed that he'd mocked her voice. She'd been so excited about meeting him. She'd planned it carefully, worked long into the night to perfect the song she was going to sing. She'd picked a dress that she'd thought made her look like a star. But he'd taken one look at her and made the same judgements as the rest of the guests at the palace party. They'd all dismissed her as some cheap, ex-footballer's daughter with nothing to offer musically.

Look at me, I'm not who you see...

The words popped into her head along with a haunting melody and despite the tense situation Izzy felt the fizz of excitement she always experienced when words and notes came together. Relieved to have something to distract her, she hummed softly as it flowed into her head like magic.

Deep inside there's someone else, longing to break free...

'You ruin your sister's evening and you're still singing? Don't you know when to be quiet?'

'I did not ruin her evening.' Or had she? Izzy felt her conscience prick and then felt a ripple of concern because even through the haze of alcohol she'd been aware that her half-sister was behaving oddly.

With a stab of regret, she tugged her phone out of her bag and texted one word to Allegra.
Sorry.

But her family should be sorry too, she thought. They never took her seriously. *I'm not what you see, don't turn away...* Terrified that she might forget it, she closed her eyes and hummed it a few times, forcing it into her memory. The tune and the words blurred as her mind drifted. The deep purr of the engine became soothing background noise....

She awoke with a start and realised that they were driving along an avenue, the trees flanking the road providing a menacing guard of honour. Groggy, she turned her head. 'I fell asleep.'

He pressed his foot to the accelerator. *'Non c'è problema.* You were silent. A vast improvement. And talking of silence, don't use your phone while you're with me.'

'Now you're telling me who I can call?'

'No, I'm telling you not to call from your own phone.' He spoke with exaggerated patience. 'When we arrive at the palazzo, you can call anyone you like from a secure line. That's if anyone is still speaking to you after tonight's debacle.'

Izzy, who had no clue what a debacle was, decided that if it was linked to the engagement party it couldn't possibly be anything she'd want to repeat. She made a mental note to load a dictionary app onto her phone later. 'I sent one text to Allegra.'

'Don't send any more. You can call your mother from the palazzo.'

'Why would I want to do that?'

'I assume she'll be worried about you. Wondering where you've gone.'

'She won't even notice.' Izzy spoke without thinking and then caught his searching glance. That was the danger of drink, she thought woozily. It brought your emotions right to the surface. 'So all this "don't use your mobile" stuff—you're one of those people who believes in conspiracy theories?'

'No, I'm one of those people who has had his phone tapped.'

'Seriously? People listened in to your conversations? Were you saying something salacious at the time?' Pleased with herself for having managed to worm such an impressive word into the conversation, she wriggled deeper into the luxurious seat. She'd show him that he wasn't the only one who could use long words. 'They can listen to my conversations if they want to. I hope they're shocked. I don't care what the media say about me.'

'Of course you don't.' His derisory tone was a long way from complimentary. 'You were created by the media. You depend on them for your survival. You obviously love the press and everything they can do for you.'

His biting assessment of her situation was like

a hard slap, all the more painful because it was partly true. She didn't love the press, *that* wasn't true, but she was savvy enough to know that publicity made a difference. It had taken her a year of hard knocks to learn that the press was not her friend. She knew now that just because they called her 'Izzy' and acted as if they were on her side, they weren't.

The notes faded from Izzy's brain, as did the excitement of writing a new song.

It had been a crazy fantasy to think Prince Matteo, friend to rock stars and royalty, would listen to her singing and be impressed. 'You're entitled to your opinion about the press, but don't *ever* think you know me.'

Look at me, I'm not who you see.

Suddenly she wished she hadn't worn the strawberry sequin dress. She'd been so excited about it when she'd noticed it in the store. It had been the sexiest dress she'd seen and when she'd tried it on she'd thought she looked like a popstar. But when she thought about the elegant, restrained clothes everyone else had worn she realised that she'd got it wrong again. She'd stood out for all the wrong reasons.

Izzy blinked rapidly as she remembered the

condescending glances and the barely concealed smirks. It would have taken more than the right dress to make her fit in. Her whole look was wrong. She didn't have a slim, aristocratic face like so many of the women at the engagement party. Her cheeks were round and her nose turned up at the end. They had smooth, perfect hair. Hers insisted on curling. Theirs was golden or glossy brown—hers looked as if she'd rolled in a vat of strawberries. At school she'd been given a detention for colouring her hair and no amount of protestation on her part had convinced the headmistress that Izzy Jackson had developed pink streaks in her hair at the age of three. Apparently her grandmother's hair had been the same.

Most of the time she told herself that she didn't care. But creative, dreamy Izzy, for all her bounce and outgoing nature, was extremely sensitive.

Look at me, I'm not who you see,

Deep inside there's someone else, longing to break free...

Maybe there were advantages to being forced to hide out at his palazzo, she mused.

She could just work on her song until it was perfect. She'd write something so amazing that people *had* to listen. And maybe, just maybe, she could persuade the Prince of Darkness to at least let her help with the final preparations for the Rock 'n' Royal concert. Perhaps he'd even get her a ticket!

Cheered by that thought, Izzy allowed herself a tiny dream where she was backstage chatting with her favourite stars.

Every year since she was a teenager she'd watched the concert live on TV. The event was giant, backed by his friend the famous music producer Hunter Capshaw, who was a genius at staging live events. She'd read that the two of them already had the biggest names in the industry signed up and willing to donate their time for such a good cause. Rock royalty. Not national jokes, like her.

Without thinking, Izzy slid her hand to her hem and tried to tug her dress a little further down her thighs.

The prince caught the movement and his head turned, his dark gaze flitting over her.

Their eyes met briefly.

Heart pounding, she found herself looking at the sensual curve of his mouth and for a fleeting, unsettling second she had a wild impulse to lean forward and kiss him just to see how it felt.

Shaken by the intensity of that sexual connection, she looked away quickly.

The man had no sense of fun and he was so maddeningly sure of himself she wanted to punch him. Having never before wanted to punch someone and kiss them at the same time, Izzy decided that she must be more drunk than she'd first thought.

She tried telling herself that arrogance wasn't attractive but even so she was sneaking looks at the dusky shadow roughening his jaw and the width of those powerful shoulders.

Seriously disturbed by her own thoughts, Izzy wriggled to the furthest edge of her seat and hoped that her reaction was somehow linked with the volume of champagne she'd consumed because being stupid about a man definitely wasn't one of her goals. She'd already made that mistake and she never, ever made the same mistake twice.

'So is it always like that?'

'Like what?'

'Royal events.' She thought about the frozen features, the restrained behaviour. 'About as much fun as holding a party in a cemetery, although come to think of it lots of the women did look like skeletons. Why wasn't there any proper food?'

'There were canapés.'

'Which no one was eating. No one was doing anything except standing around looking like wax models of themselves. What's the point of a party if no one enjoys themselves? No one let themselves go.'

'You more than compensated for the rest of the guests.'

She shot him a defiant look but shame oozed through the defiance because underneath the alcohol-induced high she knew she'd behaved badly. The crazy thing was, she hadn't meant to.

'I didn't realise it was a crime to enjoy yourself at a party. So doesn't anyone ever have a good time at a royal event? With your never-ending budget you ought to be throwing the best parties in town.'

'Royal events are for other people.'

They were out of the city now, and speeding down a narrow road that started to climb.

Izzy realised she didn't have a clue where they were going. This was her first visit to the small Mediterranean principality of Santina and she knew nothing about the geography.

'What do you mean "for other people"?'

'We don't hold, or attend, events for our own entertainment. There's always a reason. A state visit, to support a charity, to thank a section of the community, to show we're interested—' he shifted gear and accelerated out of a sharp bend '—there's a never-ending list of reasons.'

'And tonight was the engagement of your brother and my sister.'

'Yes.'

Hearing something in his voice she leapt to the defence of her sister. 'He's lucky to have Allegra. She's worth a hundred of those judgemental, stuck-up skinny women back at that party.' She'd expected her hotheaded defence of her family to draw a sarcastic response but this time when he turned his head there was no sign of condescension or arrogance.

'I hope you're right because Alex can't afford for this to go wrong. None of us can.' He focused on the road again but the frown stayed on his face. 'Did anything seem strange to you about the engagement?'

'Apart from the fact my sister must be mad to marry a prince? No. Why?'

The pause was fractional. 'No reason.'

'Clearly there is a reason or you wouldn't have asked the question.' Although her head was spinning, Izzy felt a flash of unease. 'Allegra would never marry him if she didn't love him. And he must love her back or he wouldn't marry her.'

'You think love conquers all?' This time his smile was sardonic. 'How old are you?'

Stung by the mockery, Izzy gritted her teeth. It didn't matter what she said or did, he still managed to make her feel small. 'Old enough to know that you and I trapped together is a recipe for disaster. And just for the record I think love is the *only* reason to get married. There is no other reason.' She thought about her parents and then immediately pushed the thought away because the reality of their marriage clashed so badly with her own ideals. If she ever reached the point when she was ready for another relationship then she was going to do everything differently.

The prince kept his eyes on the road. 'So you believe in fairy tales?'

'I didn't say that. I said I believed in love, although just for the record I think it's hard to find. Also for the record I'd like to say that you are the most cynical guy I've ever met and you have an unfortunate tendency to stereotype everyone at first glance. Now just drop me off in the next village and I'll find myself somewhere to stay. That way we just might not kill each other.'

'We just drove through the last village. There is nowhere to drop you.'

'What village?' Izzy turned her head to look over her shoulder and then wished she hadn't as her brain suddenly felt fuzzy. 'I saw two houses. Or was it one house and I have double vision?'

'For the rest of your stay you are drinking water.'

'Just as long as you have a nice slice of stale bread to go with it.' But Izzy was starting to realise that her stay with the prince wasn't likely to be diluted by the presence of other people. 'When you said you lived miles from anywhere you weren't joking.'

'I rarely joke.'

She looked at his black dinner jacket. 'I thought you were in the air force. Why aren't you wearing a fancy uniform?'

'I left active service five years ago. Now I advise the DD.'

'DD?' She tried to get her spinning brain round it. 'Dear Daughter?'

His jaw tightened. 'Defence Department.'

'Oh. Cool.' Izzy peered into the darkness and saw nothing but tall cypress trees and olive groves. 'So do you spend a lot of time here?'

'As much as I can. I value my privacy.' His eyes

glittered with a dark emotion that was alien to her. There were dark layers to the man that were hidden away, buried deep beneath a royal exterior that no observer was allowed to penetrate.

Izzy recognised instinctively how complex he was and the gulf between them widened because she knew that she wasn't at all complex.

Her school report came to mind.

Isabelle is as shallow as a bird bath but is unlikely to provide even that useful service unless she gives up dreams of stardom and attempts to make something of her life.

She'd been determined to prove them wrong but so far she wasn't making much progress.

'Look, I'll just phone a taxi or something when we get to your place,' she muttered. 'It would be better for both of us. I can take care of myself.'

'You'll stay at my palazzo until I've decided what to do with you.'

Like a piece of rubbish, Izzy thought, that needed recycling. Which bin do I throw her in? Plastics or green waste? 'Right, because we both know I'm really going to fit in there. I can't think of anything I'd love more than being trapped somewhere isolated with just you for company.' Her singsong response was supposed to conceal how hurt she was but she saw his eyes narrow speculatively.

'I wouldn't have thought a woman who chose to wear a strapless dress made from nothing but sequins cared too much about fitting in.'

'Well, that shows you know nothing about women.'

'Funnily enough I thought I knew a great deal about women. Apparently I was wrong.' His voice was a lazy masculine drawl and her spine tingled.

'If the women there tonight are the sort you've been mixing with it's no wonder you're ignorant. They weren't really women. They didn't smile or laugh, except when they were laughing at me,' she muttered, 'and frankly I'm fed up with being the butt of everyone's humour. That's why I'd rather you dropped me off here. Let's face it, we have nothing in common. I'll just mess up your precious palazzo and although I'm pretty robust all this frowning disapproval is starting to get to me. I don't want to leave the island with confidence issues.'

He shot her a look. 'I cannot imagine you suffering from confidence issues.'

'You'd be surprised,' Izzy said darkly. 'Sometimes I feel as though the whole world is frowning at me. Like now, for instance. You keep looking at my dress as if you can't quite believe your eyes. You're obviously deeply prejudiced towards sequins.'

'They're not exactly subtle.'

'So? I love this dress.' She refused to apologise for it. 'And it's hypocritical of you to be superior given all the bling you royals own.'

He shifted gears, that strong male hand alarmingly close to her knee. 'I own "bling"?'

'Did you see that sparkly tiara thing your mother was wearing this evening?'

'That "tiara thing" was a gift from a sixteenth century British monarch.'

'Well, it was sparklier than anything I own so it's a bit hypocritical of everyone to turn their noses up at my love of shiny things just because some of us can't afford the real thing. A party *needs* sparkle and yours didn't have anywhere near enough. Talking of which, you do realise that I don't have any luggage, don't you? So unless you happen to own something that might fit me I'm going to be wearing this not-exactly-subtle dress every day I'm in captivity.'

'You are not in captivity.'

'So I can leave whenever I like?'

There was a brief pause. 'No. The focus needs to be on my brother and your sister. Not you.'

'So I *am* in captivity.'

'Consider it a holiday. You were planning to stay in the hotel for a week. We've merely altered the destination and I can assure you that the coastline around my palazzo is stunning. My staff are currently in the process of transferring your luggage—please tell me you own something that doesn't sparkle.' His gaze flickered to hers and she felt as though all the oxygen had been sucked from the air because there was something in that look that made her stomach flip.

Even without a smile on his face he was indecently, impossibly sexy.

'Do pyjamas count?' It was a good job she could never fall for a man without a sense of humour, Izzy thought shakily, otherwise she'd be in deep trouble. And she'd thought she'd been too badly hurt to even look at a man again. It was the champagne. *Surely* it was the champagne.

'Your pyjamas are the only clothes you own that don't sparkle?' His gaze skidded to hers and she turned scarlet, wishing she'd never mentioned pyjamas.

Tension throbbed between them and Izzy bit

back a wild laugh because even she recognised that the attraction between them was beyond inconvenient. And she didn't welcome it any more than he did. Her last relationship had been an utter disaster, the fallout from it played out across the world's media. She had no intention of providing more relationship fodder for public entertainment.

What might have happened next she had no idea because a pair of enormous gates manned by armed security guards swung open and the car sped through the gates without slowing down. Impressed in spite of herself, Izzy sat tensely as they sped down a tree-lined avenue that eventually opened out into a magnificent courtyard dominated by an illuminated fountain.

Ahead of them, floodlit against the star-studded Mediterranean sky, stood the palazzo, centuries old and a vision of warm honey-coloured stone.

Izzy thought of her room in her parents' mock Tudor house in England and gulped. '*This* is your home?'

'Yes. Why?'

Because it was enormous. 'It's just a bit small and pokey, that's all. I was expecting something a *lot* more magnificent. If you're trying to impress the girls then you probably need to think about trading up.' She could have sworn that his mouth finally flickered at the corners but maybe it was just wishful thinking because there was no humour in his response.

'Endeavour to behave yourself in front of my staff.'

'I thought you lived alone.'

'I do, but I have a permanent staff of fifty.'

'I hate to tell you this but a permanent staff of fifty doesn't constitute "alone." You seriously need fifty staff?' She digested that fact in amazement. 'I guessed you'd be hard work but not *that* much work. That's an awful lot of people to pick up after you. You must be terribly untidy.'

He brought the car to an abrupt halt. 'My charity is run from here with a permanent staff of ten. I also host visiting heads of state and senior government officials in my role as advisor to the Defence Department, so I require staff for that. The rest are involved with the running of the palazzo, including a team of gardeners and an archivist. I do have a private secretary, but I "pick up" after myself. And here's a friendly tip—while you're here I expect you to conduct yourself with dignity and propriety.'

'You use an *awful* lot of long words. The moment I get a signal I'm going to download a dictionary app to my phone so that I can understand you.'

His jaw tightened. 'Isabelle—'

The name made her shudder. 'Here's a friendly tip for *you*—if you want me to behave myself, *don't* call me Isabelle. It brings out the worst in me.'

Before he could respond, someone opened the car door and Izzy stepped out gratefully, the platform sole of her shoe-boots crunching on the drive. The air was fresh and cool. 'Oh, I can hear the sea. That's nice.'

'The palazzo is built on a cliff. My ancestor didn't much trust his fellow humans so he chose a position that was easily defended. Don't go wandering at night, especially after a drink.'

'I don't usually drink.'

His scathing glance suggested he didn't believe her. 'Areas of the cliff edge are crumbling. We have a major restoration project going on but with a place this size it's a never-ending battle.' The prince switched to his own language to speak to his staff and Izzy wished she'd concentrated more at school because she had no clue what he was saying.

That was another app she was going to have to download.

Italian for beginners.

But she didn't need an app to see how warmly the staff greeted him. Whatever his faults, the prince was clearly loved by those around him.

Presumably he'd delivered some sort of command because a uniformed member of the prince's household greeted her formally. 'If you would like to follow me, *signorina*.'

'Absolutely. Completely on my best behaviour at all times.' Saluting Matteo and trying desperately to walk in a straight line, Izzy staggered on her towering heels through the gilded doors and was instantly dazzled by the grandeur of the place. She stopped dead, her head tilted back as she stared at the ornate ceiling. 'Wow. Another incredible ceiling.'

'It's called a fresco.' Matteo's voice came from behind her. 'It was painted by a contemporary of Michelangelo.'

Izzy raised her eyebrows. 'How on earth did they do that without getting paint in their eyes? Last time I painted my bedroom wall I covered myself with the stuff. I had blue hair for weeks.'

'They used scaffolding.' The prince's eyes lingered on her hair. 'And the artist didn't lie on his back, he simply tilted his head.'

'And used non-drip paint. I like it.' Izzy stared at the ceiling again, slightly alarmed to see it shifting and spinning. 'I particularly like the way they've made it move.'

With a soft curse the prince caught her as she fell and scooped her up into his arms. As one of her shoes fell to the floor, she made an abortive grab for it.

'My shoe!'

'Next time don't drink so much...' This close she could see the dark shadow of his jaw and the perfect lines of his undeniably sexy mouth.

'I didn't drink too much. I just didn't eat enough and that's down to your lousy hospitality. You starve your guests. I guess that's one way of making sure they don't outstay their welcome.' Horribly dizzy, she let her head flop against his shoulder and gave a low moan as he strode towards the elegant staircase. 'This time it would be great if you could walk smoothly.'

His grip tightened on her. 'Izzy Jackson, you are a disaster.'

'I know, I know, but the tragedy is I don't mean

to be. All I wanted to do was sing,' Izzy mumbled, her face buried in hard muscle. 'But no one wanted to listen. Poor me.'

CHAPTER THREE

WONDERING how he'd come to be carrying her yet again, Matteo strode into the turret bedroom and kicked the door shut behind him.

Depositing her in the centre of the bed he stepped backwards and undid the collar of his shirt, hoping to relieve the tightness in his throat.

Izzy gave a low moan and rolled over the bed, her arms flopping above her head as she tried to focus on him.

Matteo watched her efforts to rouse herself with barely concealed anger.

Why the hell had he done this to himself?

He should have let her sabotage the party. He should have left her there and just cleared up the mess afterwards. Or let Alex deal with it himself. Anything would have been better than putting himself in this situation.

She blinked and looked around her. 'Where am I?'

Sleeping Beauty, Matteo thought grimly, *but a thousand times more lethal.*

'You are in the turret bedroom.'

'So you're locking me in the tower just like the fairy tale. But how is the prince ever going to find me here? I hope he has sat nav fitted to his horse.' Giggling, she rolled onto her side, the movement pushing her dress further up her thighs. 'Rapunzel, Rapunzel, let down your golden hair, but not if it has strawberry streaks in it because no one wants a girl with strawberry streaks.'

Matteo tried to ignore the burn of lust that ripped through him. *She had incredible legs.* 'This is our best guest suite, usually reserved for visiting royalty. It's more than you deserve.' Keeping one eye on her to make sure she didn't fall off the bed, he snatched up the phone and ordered a pot of black coffee and food, well aware that his midnight order would trigger yet more speculation from his already fascinated staff.

As someone who conducted his relationships with utmost discretion, he knew that having someone like Izzy in his home would create a huge stir.

As he ended the call she sat up and slid shakily off the bed. She stood for a moment and wobbled slightly, testing that her legs would hold her.

Bending over she pulled off her remaining shoe and almost fell. 'Oops. Champagne really affects your balance.'

'It has never affected mine.'

'That's because you're horribly, boringly controlled.'

Matteo gritted his teeth. 'Sit down.'

'Not a good idea. My head is spinning.'

'*Per meraviglia*, you are incorrigible.' He grabbed her arms to stop her falling and she swayed and flopped against him, sighing into his chest.

'I like it here. You smell *so* good.'

And she *felt* good. Soft. Fragile. Without those towering heels she was surprisingly petite. Matteo tensed his body, instinctively rejecting the effects of that knowledge because the alternative was unthinkable. 'Behave yourself.' He forced himself to release her, but she stayed welded to his chest and the contact sent a rush of heat across his skin.

'If you weren't so moody you'd be *really* sexy.' She tilted her head back and those bewitching eyes fixed on his. 'Why don't you ever smile? Are you unhappy, Matt?' That mass of soft hair whispered gently over his hand—the same hand he'd been fighting *not* to plant in the centre of her back.

He started to withdraw, but a curl of hair wound itself around his finger like a silken noose and suddenly, instead of letting go, his hand was touching her cheek. Control was eclipsed by raw desire and Matteo captured her face in his hands, bringing his mouth down on hers. Her shock mirrored his own and then her lips parted under the demands of his, her mouth soft, sweet and unapologetically sexual as she kissed him back. As her tongue slid over his, raw sexual heat ripped through him and Matteo locked his hands on her hips and pulled her hard against him.

They were welded together, their mouths creating a fire that devoured both of them, so wild and out of control that the next move would have been the bed behind them had it not been for the knock on the door.

He heard it dimly, through a fog of sexual excitement and primitive need, but when he tried to lift his head she gave a low moan of protest and dug her fingers into his hair, prolonging the kiss for a few more erotic moments. Or maybe he was the one who prolonged the kiss. Either way they were still kissing when the second knock came, louder this time, followed by the unmistakable sound of the doorknob turning.

With a supreme effort Matteo dragged his mouth from hers and disengaged himself just moments before one of the kitchen staff entered with a tray of food and a pot of coffee.

Twice, he thought. Twice in the space of a few hours he'd lost control with this woman.

'*Grazie.* Just leave it on the table.'

If the girl from his kitchens was surprised by his unusually abrupt tone then she didn't show it. Instead she simply took the cover off the sandwiches and was about to pour the coffee when Matteo dismissed her.

'I'll do it.'

The girl scurried out of the room.

Next to him Izzy stood, swaying slightly on her bare feet, her eyes not quite meeting his.

She looked slightly dazed, as if she'd been struck by lightning.

He knew exactly how she was feeling only he didn't have alcohol as an excuse.

'Eat something.'

She stirred and looked round her. 'What happened to my bag?' She spied it on the bed and walked unsteadily over to it. 'Need to write something down before I forget.' It took her three attempts to unclip the bag and pull out a pen and a small notebook.

Matteo watched in exasperation as she tried to focus on something she'd written.

'What are you doing?'

'I'm evaluating today. I do it every night before I go to sleep, but I'm afraid that tonight I'm going to forget, so I'm doing it now.'

'Evaluating today?'

'Every day should have a purpose.' She swayed and almost lost her balance and Matteo was just stepping forward ready to catch her when she planted her hands on the bed to steady herself. The notebook fell to the floor and he retrieved it, his temper simmering.

He was about to hand it back and make his exit when he saw the words on the page.

Goal of the Day—Meet Moody Matteo.

A scalding flame of anger speared his body. 'You actually took the trouble to write it down?'

'Give me that—it's private.' Her attempt to snatch the book from him almost sent her tumbling again. 'And yes, I write it down. It's like making a promise to myself. I *will* achieve my dream.'

Feeling sick to his stomach, Matteo handed her

the book. 'I'm going to kill that dream of yours stone dead. Get this straight right now—I am *not* your goal.' His palms were damp and the past flashed into his head with explosive force, blasting through the barriers he erected between himself and the world. 'I am *not* your target.'

She winced. 'Could you speak in a softer voice? My head hurts. And I do think you're slightly overreacting.'

Matteo swore fluently in Italian and strode to the door.

Her voice stopped him. 'Well, this has been a very interesting evening. I think we've each learned something about the other, which is useful as we're going to be related. I've learned that despite being so uptight on the surface, underneath you're steaming hot and you kiss like a god. What have you learned, Your Highness?'

He'd learned that what had happened to him years before remained embedded like shrapnel in his subconscious.

He'd learned that his control was a much more fragile thing than he'd believed.

He'd learned that helping his brother was going to cost him dearly.

'I've learned never to carry a woman to bed

when she's drunk. Go and take a cold shower and sleep it off. And try not to drown. *A domani.*'

Izzy woke with a crushing headache, a mouth as dry as a child's sandbox and a clear memory of every single thing that had happened the night before. Why, oh, why, couldn't she just have forgotten everything? Why wasn't she one of those people who could never remember a thing that had happened? A bit of alcohol-induced amnesia would have been extremely welcome because most of the memories weren't good ones.

She remembered being starving-hungry. She remembered grabbing the microphone at the party and being showered by disapproving stares. And she remembered the adrenalin rush of being driven by the prince in his super sports car.

And the kiss…

Closing her eyes, she gave a moan.

Oh, yes, she remembered the kiss. And she had a feeling she'd still be able to remember it when she was ninety and wrinkled. Where on earth had someone so zipped up and restrained as the Prince of Darkness learned to kiss like that? Except that he hadn't been zipped up and restrained when he'd kissed her. One moment he'd been cold and disapproving; the next he'd been giving a crash course in the true meaning of sexual excitement. Because she knew that what they'd shared had nothing to do with romance and everything to do with hot physical chemistry.

She'd been kissed before, but never like that— never had the feelings spread all the way through her body creating a craving so powerful she hadn't seen the benefit in stopping. Who in their right mind would want to stop something that felt so good?

And the craving was still there…

Shaken by feelings she didn't recognise, she decided that the first thing to do was fix the throb in her head. Reaching for the jug of water by the bed, she noticed a pool of scarlet sequins on the floor. She dimly remembered wriggling out of her dress and then flopping onto the bed.

'Never again,' she moaned as she poured water into a glass and drank. 'Never again am I drinking champagne with nothing to eat.'

Gingerly, trying not to move her head too vigorously, she squinted at her watch.

Ten-thirty.

She never slept in. Ever. She set her alarm for

seven every morning no matter what she'd done the day before.

Wincing, she eased herself gently off the bed and padded into the bathroom feeling like road-kill.

Raccoon eyes stared back at her where her make-up had run, her face was horribly pale and she had a red mark on her cheek where she'd slept awkwardly. 'No wonder he wasn't keen to hang around.' As she wiped away the damage, she noticed that although the palazzo was ancient and historic, there was nothing ancient or historic about her bedroom, or the luxurious bathroom with its walk-in shower.

In fact, the palazzo was more opulent and pala-tial than anywhere she'd stayed in her life.

Outside, the sun was blazing, and despite the headache her spirits lifted. The Mediterranean weather was a pleasant change from dreary, show-ery London.

Determined not to have a completely wasted day, Izzy picked up her pen and scribbled on a new page of her notebook.

Goal of the Day—Finish writing 'Look at Me.'

At some point her suitcase had been delivered and someone had unpacked her few clothes and hung them in the dressing room. Trying not to notice how lonely her dresses looked in that enormous space, Izzy grabbed her favourite denim shorts and a pink top and dressed quickly. Then she retrieved her suitcase, hunted in one of the concealed pockets and pulled out her battered teddy bear.

Clearing her throat, she propped him up against the pillows. 'Right. Are you listening? I need to finish this song and you're the nearest thing to an enthusiastic audience I'm ever going to get in this world. At least you don't heckle.'

She hummed, sang scales and did her usual vocal exercises to warm up her voice but today her enthusiasm for her music was seriously dented by her pounding head. Conscious that not to achieve her one simple goal was a slippery slope towards giving up, she persevered until she was reasonably satisfied with the lyrics and the melody.

Deciding that what she needed following that was fresh air, she was about to leave the room when there was a knock on the door and a girl entered carrying a tray.

'*Buongiorno, signorina.* His Highness thought you might be hungry as you missed breakfast.'

Izzy's stomach rolled. Great. When she wanted

food there was none to be had, and when she didn't… 'Thanks.' Not wanting to offend, she managed a weak smile. 'That's kind of you.'

The girl smiled dreamily. 'His Highness is an incredibly thoughtful person.'

Remembering his iron grip as he'd dragged her away from the stage and his non-stop flow of sarcastic observations, Izzy begged to differ, but the girl couldn't have been more than eighteen years old and obviously thought the prince walked on water.

Who was she to shatter someone's illusions?

'He's a gem, no doubt about that.' And moody. And sexy. And complicated. Cold and distant one minute and scorching hot and wildly passionate the next. It was enough to give a girl emotional whiplash. 'I'm sure he's kind to old ladies and children.'

The girl beamed back, delighted to welcome someone else into the Prince Matteo fan club. 'He *is*. He raises so much money for charity and he knows *everyone*, of course. He just has to pick up the phone and the next minute a child is spending the day with their football hero.'

'That's great.' Actually, it wasn't great because she didn't want to have a positive opinion of him. 'So where is he now?'

'His Highness is in back-to-back meetings all morning but he asked that you join him for lunch at twelve-thirty in the Rose dining room. It overlooks the English rose garden on the south side of the palazzo.' The girl hesitated, excitement dancing in her eyes. 'You're the first woman he's allowed to stay overnight. We're all so excited.'

Feeling like a fraud, Izzy ushered the girl to the door, remembering the delight the staff had shown at his arrival the night before. Clearly Moody Matteo must have hidden depths if he managed to inspire such devotion in the people who worked for him.

Walking over to the windows she stared down at the grounds. Acres of formal gardens stretched beneath her and Izzy stared in fascination because she'd never seen so much green space. Perfectly manicured hedges, a long sweep of grass and at the bottom an ornamental lake with a central fountain.

Heat pricked the back of her neck and she suddenly realised that it really was very warm.

She had two hours to kill before lunch.

And she knew exactly how she was going to spend it.

* * *

The day had started badly and was becoming worse with each email and phone call.

It didn't help that his mind wasn't focused on work, but wrapped up in an erotic daydream involving a woman in shimmering red sequins with strawberry-streaked hair.

He had no idea what it was about her that had smashed through his control. Yes, she was pretty, but he met beautiful women every day of the week. Women more elegant, more refined in their tastes, more decorous in their behaviour. By comparison, Izzy was wild.

He closed his eyes and told himself that wild wasn't good.

Especially when he'd been her Goal of the Day.

Being the target of female attention for all the wrong reasons was one of the penalties of being a prince but he'd never met anyone quite as blatant as her.

Maybe it was her presence in his home that was having this effect on him. He never, ever allowed women to stay the night here. It was too…personal.

'Nice voice.' His PA slapped a pile of papers on his desk and Matteo looked up at her blankly.

'Pardon?'

'Your guest. The windows are open and she's been singing. You put her in the turret bedroom, didn't you?' There was curiosity in her eyes. 'If she's going to be part of the concert you'd better tell me what—'

'She isn't part of the concert,' Matteo snapped, and then felt an immediate flash of guilt as he saw curiosity turn to shock. 'Sorry.'

'That's all right. It's always stressful just before the big day, although it's not like you to let it get to you. Nor is it like you to have overnight female guests while you're here.' She placed a cup of coffee next to the papers. 'So will Miss Jackson be—?'

'Miss Jackson isn't part of anything we do here. Did Hunter call?'

'While you were on the phone. He's calling you back in ten minutes.'

'Right.' Matteo stood and prowled over to the window, restless and unsettled.

Why the hell was she still singing when no one could hear her?

He turned back to his PA, trying to delete images of Izzy Jackson from his brain. 'The concert is just weeks away and we still haven't found the right song.'

'I know. Cue our annual nervous breakdown. I've been emailing Callie, but her assistant says she just isn't inspired since her relationship with Rock Dog broke up. She's taking some time out to "fill her creative well."'

Matteo ground his teeth. 'And how long is that expected to take?'

'She spent last week in a secret location in Arizona. This is the usual pattern when she breaks up with someone.'

Dragging himself out of an erotic rerun of the previous night's kiss, Matteo returned to his desk and opened up his laptop. 'Remind me why we chose her to write and perform our charity single?'

'Because her last single was the fastest download ever. But she was in love when she wrote it so she was inspired.'

'And the single before that?'

'She was in love then too. Different guy.'

Love, Matteo thought savagely, had a lot to answer for.

I believe in love, I just think it's hard to find. Izzy's words came back into his head and he frowned, thinking it was an unusually observant comment from someone so superficial.

'We can't wait for Callie to be inspired so we'd better move to plan B. Get Pete Foster on the phone.'

He worked for the rest of the morning and by the time he'd unravelled one crisis after another he was cursing creative people whose approach to work was so unreliable.

He'd left instructions that Izzy should meet him for lunch, but when he finally made it to the dining room the table was laid but the room was empty apart from two flustered footmen, one of whom was sneaking looks out of the window as Matteo strode into the room.

'Where is she?' Matteo addressed the senior of the two, a man who had worked for him for more than ten years.

'I believe Miss Jackson went for a walk, Your Highness.' The fact that the man didn't quite meet his gaze confirmed his suspicions that Izzy Jackson was doing something she shouldn't.

'Do you have any idea *where*?'

The gaze of the younger of the two men slid towards the window and then back again. 'She's… outside, Sir.'

'*Where* outside?' Matteo's tone was lethally soft and the man's cheeks flushed.

'I believe she's gone for a walk down to the lake, Sir. She said she was too hot.'

Sensing that there was a great deal more that he wasn't being told, Matteo spun on his heel.

He had a mountain of work problems waiting for his attention, the last thing he needed was to be chasing some wannabe popstar round his grounds. If they were going to share living space then she had to learn to respect boundaries.

Deeply regretting the impulse that had driven him to bring her to his home and even more deeply regretting the impulse that had driven him to kiss her, Matteo strode through the grounds of the palazzo.

He never allowed a woman to get under his skin but somehow she'd managed it.

He could see no sign of her anywhere and was about to try the botanical garden when he heard singing and a splash of colour caught his eye. Turning his head, he stared down the long sweep of grass to the ornamental lake that could be seen from the front of the palazzo and formed the focus of the Renaissance garden. In the centre of the lake was the famous Neptune fountain and there, splashing happily around in the spray, was Izzy.

Finally he understood the unusual buzz amongst his staff.

Never had the formal gardens of the palazzo been used for such a practical purpose.

Teeth gritted, blood boiling, Matteo strode down the grassy slope towards the lake. As he approached he noticed a small pile of clothes and what looked like the remains of her breakfast, a half-eaten croissant on a plate.

Apparently she hadn't noticed him and she twirled in the fountain, sending droplets of water flying. Her strawberry-pink hair clung wet to her bare shoulders and the only thing covering her modesty were two skimpy pieces of a bright fuchsia bikini.

She was a blur of colour, brighter than any bloom in the formal gardens, and in that moment he knew that if he'd been an artist, this was the image he would have chosen to paint.

Girl in a fountain.

He saw lush breasts pushing at the top of her bikini, a smooth flat stomach and dazzling smile momentarily stopped him in his tracks, as she sang and splashed with unselfconscious enjoyment.

Even when she finally noticed him, her smile didn't slip. '*Buongiorno*, Your Highness.'

'What the hell are you doing?'

'Relaxing! This is amazing. Like having your own shower in a swimming pool. *So* cool. Is this Michelangelo again? The guy really knows how to build a great statue. I love everything about him. It would be a great place to film a music video.'

'Get out of there right now.' His icy tone slid off her like the water from the fountain, his unconcealed disapproval having no apparent effect on her exuberance. 'Are you listening to me?'

'I'm just cooling down. I had a bit of a headache and you did tell me to take a cold shower. Great advice by the way.'

'That was last night.'

'Better late than never and it proves I *do* listen to you. Why are you wearing a suit? Aren't you slightly overdressed for the weather? It's boiling.'

Matteo kept his eyes fixed on her face and resisted the temptation to wipe the sweat from the back of his neck. 'I've had meetings this morning. I'm working.'

'Oh. Poor you.' She flipped back her hair and dipped her hands in the cool water. 'So if you're working, what are you doing here? You should be focusing.'

She was telling *him* about focus?

'You were supposed to join me for lunch.'

A wry little smile tugged at her mouth. 'We both know you didn't really *want* me to join you for lunch. You were just fulfilling your duty and I don't want to be anyone's duty. It was bad enough watching you leaving the party early last night, sacrificing yourself on "Izzy removal duty." Frankly I couldn't stand the thought of sitting in that stuffy room indoors trying to work out which fork to use and which glass to drink out of and feeling generally stupid while you give me *that* look. Anyway, this is perfect picnic weather. I brought the rest of my breakfast outside. Help yourself. Your chef is a genius. Those pastries are homemade.'

'I don't eat picnics.'

'Seriously? Eating outdoors beats a five-star restaurant every time.' Her eyes brimmed with humour. 'Take off that jacket and sit down on the grass. Relax. Try and look as if you're enjoying yourself. Who knows—you might actually have some fun.'

Matteo found himself paralyzed because her words took his mind spinning back to a time he'd managed to put behind him.

Let's have some fun, Matteo. Forget you're a prince...

His jaw clenched. These days he never forgot who he was. Never. 'Get out of the fountain. Now.'

'Why? I like it here. And you're very bad-tempered this morning.'

'I'm not asking you again.'

'Good, because I can't *stand* nagging. If you want me out, you'll have to come and get me.' Her smile didn't slip but there was a challenge in her eyes and he resisted the temptation to do exactly as she'd suggested. She'd be slippery under his hands. Wet. She'd feel—

Incredible.

'Isabelle...'

'Oops. *Big* mistake. Warned you about that last night. *Never* call me Isabelle. It brings out the worst in me.' Her fingers skimmed the surface of the water and her eyes met his. Something wicked gleamed there. 'Now you're in trouble, Your Highness.'

Reading her mind he breathed in sharply. 'Don't you *dare.*'

'Are you going to come in and stop me?' She was flirting with him. Not in the hopeful, con-trived way he'd witnessed all his life but in a saucy, natural, unaffected way that sent his pulse rocketing. There was something about her complete absence of deference that heated his blood.

Still, there was no way she'd—

The shower of cold water splattered his hair, his jacket and the front of his shirt, which promptly welded itself to his skin. *'Maledizione.'* He swore fluently in Italian and wiped the water from his eyes with a hand that wasn't quite steady, only to find himself showered again. 'Are you crazy? This suit is silk.'

'Better take it off then, before it's ruined.'

He did just that, shrugging the jacket from his shoulders in a violent movement and saw her gaze slide to his damp shirt.

Her lips parted and her eyelids lowered slightly. 'Nice body, Your Highness. I've never seen a ripped prince before.'

The air around them grew hotter. Matteo took a step towards the fountain.…

'Your Highness—' A breathless voice came from behind him and he dragged his eyes from a laughing, unrepentant Izzy to Serena, his cool-eyed PA, who was walking briskly down the grass towards him, her cheeks slightly pink from the heat. 'I have Hunter Capshaw for you. You weren't answering your phone.'

Matteo hadn't even heard his phone.

All his attention had been focused on the girl in the fountain.

And right now every muscle in his body was straining with the effort to resist the chemistry that pulled at them.

Izzy represented everything he avoided. Everything dangerous. Even more so since she'd admitted that getting him to notice her had been her Goal of the Day. His mood wasn't improved by the realisation that had Serena arrived a moment later he would have been in that fountain with her. He hoped he would have had the willpower to simply drag her out of the water, but after what had happened between them the night before he wasn't convinced.

'Ask him to hold. I'll take the call in my office.' He snapped out the words and then immediately felt guilty because the beam of anger should have been directed at the girl in the fountain, not Serena, and once again he was going to be forced to apologise.

His frustration mounting, he threw a furious

glance at Izzy. 'Get dressed and meet me in my office.'

She tried to pout but she was laughing too hard to pull it off. 'That doesn't sound like a whole lot of fun.'

Matteo glared at her. 'Do it.'

Then he stepped over her picnic and strode past his gawking PA, past the watchful eyes of the stone lions that had been there since the sixteenth century but had doubtless never witnessed a scene like this, and into the rooms of the palazzo that had been converted into state-of-the-art offices.

Next time, he vowed, *he'd leave trouble where he found it instead of bringing it home with him.*

CHAPTER FOUR

Izzy fidgeted on the elegant chair. Her damp hair cooled her bare neck and shoulders and a few blades of grass had stuck to her feet and now niggled uncomfortably inside her espadrilles.

The offices were bright and light, the reception area filled with towering plants and modern paintings. A contrast to all the ancient history around them.

This was supposed to be a holiday, but she felt restless and full of repressed energy. Her plan had failed so now she needed to rethink. It didn't feel *right* sitting here doing nothing when her goal was still so far out of reach. She should be planning. Writing more songs.

But it was hard writing a song without a piano.

Her foot tapped the floor impatiently and she wondered how long he was going to keep her sitting here.

'His Royal Highness will see you now.' It was the woman who had come to fetch him at the fountain. Elegant. Not a hair out of place. Not a single crease in her suit.

Feeling seriously underdressed in her denim shorts and T-shirt with *Crazy Girl* picked out in sequins, Izzy silently admired her poise. 'So, is he furious? Am I dead?'

The woman stood stiff for a moment and then her eyes slid to the door of the office, which was half closed. 'I've never seen him lose his temper,' she whispered, 'and I've worked for him for two years. What have you done to him?'

'Driven him mad. It's my special gift.' Izzy stood and walked towards the door. Bracing herself for conflict, she paused for a second and then knocked and entered.

The prince was seated behind the desk, his eyes on the computer screen.

He looked sleek, spectacularly good-looking and completely out of her league, and Izzy's heart bumped hard against her chest.

Whatever faults he might have, there was no denying that the man was truly gorgeous. *Seriously* hot. Even more so now she'd had a glimpse of what he was hiding under that formal suit.

A different suit, she noticed.

He'd changed.

She wondered what he'd look like in jeans and then decided that he'd probably look spectacular in anything. Or nothing.

Seeing him behind the large desk, formidable in every way, it was almost impossible to believe that this same man had kissed her the night before. For a fleeting second she'd felt raw, untamed passion and the contrast between that man and the restrained, controlled man she was viewing now was startling and puzzling.

In his own time he lifted his gaze and the glint in those eyes reflected her inner turmoil right back at her. 'Sit down.' He radiated control and authority and Izzy stood rigid, feeling like a schoolgirl called to the headmaster's office.

'It was just a few drops of water, for goodness' sake.' She didn't mention last night's kiss. He was in a bad enough mood without mentioning another of her transgressions. Or was it his transgression? *He'd* kissed *her*, hadn't he? And there had been nothing soft or romantic about it. His mouth had been rough and demanding, as if—

She frowned. *As if he'd been angry about something.*

And he was angry now.

There was no trace of humour in his face, no

softening of the hard angles of those aristocratic features.

'What does it take to get you to behave like a normal person?'

'Most normal people would have wanted to swim in the fountain.'

'There's a wealth of difference between wanting to do something and actually doing it.' His eyes were cold. 'Sit down!'

Cowed by his icy tone, Izzy plopped onto the chair. Without thinking, she toed off her shoes and crossed her legs under her so that she was balanced on the seat.

'You need to learn to—' He broke off as he saw the way she was sitting. 'What are you doing?'

'Sitting. You told me to sit. I sat.'

'I told you to sit, not take your shoes off.' Tension throbbed beneath the surface of his rigidly controlled frame and Izzy wondered what it took to make him relax.

'My feet hurt. That's partly your fault for dragging me miles through the palace last night and partly because you just made me run up a steep grassy bank in my espadrilles and they rub. I didn't bring hiking boots and your garden is the size of a park. This is how I sit. I'm making myself comfortable.' Eyeing him cautiously, she wondered if he was waiting for her to apologise. 'Look, I'm sorry about last night. I admit it wasn't my finest moment. And I'm sorry about your suit. Give me the cleaning bill. But you could maybe think about dressing in a more practical way.'

'Given that swimming in the fountain is not normally part of my working day, a suit is perfectly practical.' He placed his pen on the desk with exaggerated care. 'We need to agree to some boundaries while you're staying here.'

'Boundaries? Yippee.' Izzy pulled a face and then saw his expression and shrugged. 'OK. Fire away.'

'The first is that you don't swim in the fountain.'

'Why not?'

'Because it isn't designed for swimming.'

'It's water. What else do you need to swim?'

'It is an ornamental lake, designed in the seventeenth century by a famous landscape architect.' He enunciated the words carefully, as if speaking to a child. 'I open the gardens several times a year to interested visitors. The fountain is part of the tour. It's an object of interest to historians. It is *not* for bathing.'

'Then whoever designed the fountain must have

been a real tease because every normal person would automatically want to leap in it to cool down.' Catching his smouldering glare she nibbled her lip. 'Could I swim in it if I promise to leap straight out if I see a coach party coming?' His expression went from black to thunderous and she rolled her eyes. 'Right, no fountain.' She looked for a chink in his armour but there was no sign of the passionate man she'd glimpsed the night before and no trace of amusement on that hard, sensual mouth.

'There is a swimming pool on the south terrace. When we've finished here I'll show you the way.'

'I bet it doesn't have a statue of Neptune in the middle of it.'

He ignored her interruption. 'I do not expect to have to remove you half naked from the fountain. And when I ask you to do something, I expect you to comply without argument.'

'Comply. That basically means I'm supposed to do what you say.' Izzy wrinkled her nose. 'I can't promise that without knowing what it is. I mean, you might ask me to do something shocking. Or eat oysters or something disgusting like that. Ew.'

'Oysters are a delicacy.'

'They're slippery, slimy, putrid things that make me—'

'Fine! Spare me the details.' His eyes gleamed dark and promised dire punishment if she interrupted again. 'Oysters will not be on the menu, but when I ask you to join me for lunch, you'll do it.'

'The thing is, I know you don't really want me to join you. And although I appreciate the gesture, honestly it would be just too much pressure.' Izzy lifted her hand to her lips and nibbled the corner of her nails.

'Joining me for lunch is "pressure"?'

'Yes. And if you must know I *did* put my head round the dining room door fifteen minutes before I was supposed to meet you but I lost my nerve.'

Dark eyebrows rose. 'It requires nerve to enter my dining room?'

'There was a whole army of forks on the table. And knives. And four different glasses,' Izzy mumbled. 'Why on earth a person needs that much cutlery I have no idea unless you were just doing it to make me feel small. And as for the four glasses—after last night I'm just not that thirsty.'

There was a long, loaded silence.

'So you're happy to elbow your way onto the

stage and hijack the entertainment, but you won't walk into a room laid for lunch?'

'That's completely different. I sing all the time. I have confidence in my ability even if no one else does. I don't eat in formal dining rooms being stared at by dead people.'

Astonishment flickered across his face. 'Dead people?'

'All those portraits. The people are all dead, aren't they?'

'Yes, but—'

'It's very unsettling. In my house we have family photos but they're all of people who are alive. Dad, Mum, my sisters—actually, there is one of my gran and she died last year, but that doesn't count because at least I knew her. There's something *truly* weird about having nothing but dead people staring down at you.'

'I'm confused,' he drawled softly. 'Is your problem with the "dead people" or the place setting?'

'Both.'

'I refuse to remove the portraits, but I can help you navigate the glasses and cutlery. It's very easy. The simple rule is that you start at the outside and work your way in. Don't put your elbows on the table and—' he frowned at her '—*don't* bite your nails.'

'I'm supposed to use a knife and fork for that too?' But her hand dropped into her lap and she watched warily as he leaned back in his chair, his gaze disturbingly intense.

'I can't believe you were scared of my dining room.'

'Not *scared* exactly.' Izzy bristled at the thought. 'I'm not *scared* of anything. There's a big difference between scared and uncomfortable. It's just that there are all sorts of rules for eating in a place like that and I don't know any of them.'

'You didn't seem too bothered about rules when you were swimming in my fountain.'

'Are you seriously telling me you've never been tempted to swim in that fountain?'

'Never.'

'Now you're lying.' She watched him closely. 'Admit it—just for a moment back there you were tempted to get in the fountain with me. You did think about it. If your PA hadn't arrived when she did you would have taken off that suit and—'

'I would not have taken off the suit.' He snapped out the words and she stared at him, stunned by the sudden change in him. The transformation from ice cool to scorching hot was so rapid she found it unsettling.

'Right. OK. If you say so.' The whole atmosphere of the room had changed. A knot formed in her stomach and just looking at him made her heart race. She'd been trying so hard not to think about that kiss but the more she tried not to think about it, the more she thought of it.

And she knew he was thinking of it too.

Was that why he was so on edge?

For the briefest moment his gaze flickered to her mouth and then he stood abruptly. 'I have work to do.'

'Me too.' Izzy stood, objecting to the implication that she was distracting him. 'You're the one who dragged me in here. I was perfectly happy doing my own thing.'

'Your "own thing" involved swimming in my fountain. Are you capable of occupying yourself for a few hours without disrupting the place?'

'I'm not a toddler.' Izzy was about to make another quip when she saw the lines of tiredness around his eyes. Guilt pressed down on her. 'You look like you're having a really bad day. Is that because of me?' He'd been forced to bring her here, hadn't he? Her eyes slid to the stack of newspapers and she strolled over to his desk and grabbed one. 'So did they cover the party? Any news of drunk, badly behaved sisters getting thrown out?' But despite her light tone she hoped desperately that her own actions hadn't ruined her sister's engagement because that had never been her intention.

'Fortunately they seem to have focused on Alex and Allegra.'

'So you and your brother really stick together. Look out for each other.' Used to family who were monumentally selfish, Izzy flicked through the pages and tried not to feel envious of the obvious bond between the two princes. 'Oh—lovely one of Allegra's dress. And her hair looks great like that.' Was it her imagination or did her sister looked strained? She peered closer but decided that newspapers had a habit of making you look awful as she knew from bitter experience.

'Just one British newspaper decided you were more interesting than your half-sister.' He handed her a tabloid newspaper and her heart missed a beat because she could guess the headline all too easily.

This time it read *Izzy the Entertainment.*

'That could be worse.' Ignoring the stab of misery that came with each bout of public mockery,

Izzy reminded herself that being in the media spotlight was just part of what she'd signed up for and there was no point in whining about it. She put it to one side, facedown so she didn't have to look at the picture they'd chosen from their archive. 'The headlines are mostly positive and that's what you wanted. The public loves the whole prince-marries-ordinary-girl thing. So why are you frowning? Are you still mad that I swam in the fountain?'

His eyes narrowed. 'Let's just say I'm naturally suspicious of women who make me their Goal of the Day.'

'I won't apologise for having goals. I'm proud of how hard I work,' Izzy exploded in her own defence. 'I could have gone into that party with no objective other than to dance and drink which is what most people did, instead of which I knew what I wanted and I went for it.'

He leaned his hips against the desk and watched her. 'I suppose I should at least applaud your honesty.'

'You make it sound like a bad thing but that's because you have no idea what it's like to be a normal person. It's easy for you—if you speak, everyone listens. You have access to anyone and anything that interests you. Someone like me just doesn't get the opportunities. That's why I did *Singing Star*, but that turned out to be a bad move so it might not be such a great example.' Izzy bit her lip. 'I did everything I could to make you notice me. I researched what you liked but research can only tell you so much about a person.'

That confession was met by a deadly silence.

'You *researched* me?' His voice was dangerously soft. 'And what did your "research" tell you?'

'That you have eclectic tastes.' She was pleased with the word. 'And lots of people vying for your attention, of course. I knew you wouldn't be a pushover.'

'But clearly you're not daunted by a little healthy competition,' he drawled, and she stared at the glitter in his eyes, wondering what he was getting at.

'Competition is part of life. You have to ignore it. If you have a dream, it's no good giving up at the first fence. If it means that much to you, you have to keep at it. And if a plan doesn't work then you have to try another.' It sounded so much easier to say than to do, she thought, and he certainly didn't look impressed.

'So is this a Jackson family trait? Does Allegra have a Goal of the Day too?' His voice was ice cold. 'How did you agree on which prince would suit which sister?'

Izzy thought it was a strange question. 'Technically she's my half-sister and of course we didn't fight. I was only ever interested in you. For obvious reasons.'

'Enlighten me.'

She looked at him. 'Sorry?'

'I'm interested in your reasons for picking me. If I'm supposed to be your Prince Charming then I'd better be informed of the qualities you value. Or were you just living out a princess fantasy?'

Princess fantasy? Izzy stared at him blankly, rewinding the conversation in her head. Had she missed something? 'Who said anything about you being my Prince Charming?'

'If your goal is to marry me then I should at least have a basic understanding of your expectations if we're to stand any chance of living happily ever after.'

'*Marry* you?' Izzy gaped at him. 'Are you *crazy*? Whoever said anything about marrying you? I can't think of anything more horrific!'

'You made it your goal to target me. To quote you, "I was only ever interested in you."'

'Yes, but not because—' She broke off, robbed of speech as his meaning sank into her shocked brain. 'I was talking about your *music* contacts. The fact you have ultimate control over the Rock 'n' Royal concert. But you thought—' It was her turn to look stunned. 'My goal was to persuade you to give me a role in the concert. Let me get involved in some way. You have all the right contacts. I never, ever wanted to marry you! I don't want to marry anyone. That's nowhere on my list of goals—short, medium or long term!'

There was a long, tense silence and disbelief spread across his face, quickly followed by incredulity.

'You targeted me for my music contacts?'

'Yes! When Allegra invited us all to the engagement party it was just too good an opportunity to miss. My career is totally in the doldrums and then fate intervened. My goal was to impress you with my singing.' Remembering just how far she'd fallen short of that objective, her face burned.

'Accidenti.' He rubbed his fingers over his forehead. 'You're saying you thought I'd hear your voice and invite you to sing?'

'Maybe it was a little ambitious as goals go, but—'

'So you treated your sister's engagement party as an audition?'

Put like that it sounded awful and Izzy squirmed. 'Well, not exactly, because obviously I was hoping she'd enjoy the song too, but—'

'For your information we had the artists and set lists confirmed months ago. And as for inviting you to participate—' he breathed deeply '—I have never heard anything more ridiculous in my life.'

'Oh. Well, thanks for that compliment. When the other bruises to my ego have healed I'll be sure to add that one.' Her spine stiff, Izzy held his gaze and absorbed the blow the way she'd absorbed all the others in her life. 'Singing was my primary goal, but my secondary goal was just to help in some way. Get involved.'

'You thought you could help with the concert? How?'

She discovered that amusement could be more hurtful than biting sarcasm. 'Don't say it like that. Of course I'm capable of helping. I know about music. I know *a lot* about music.'

'There's not much that surprises me, but I confess I am surprised.'

'Me too! How could you be so arrogant as to assume I'd want to marry you? God, what is *wrong* with you? I don't even *know* you! And you'd be totally wrong for me. I could never be with someone who doesn't want to swim in a fountain.' She was horribly flustered and that feeling didn't fade as she watched his spectacular eyes narrow.

'It's not arrogance. It's experience. Believe me when I tell you that becoming a princess is the pinnacle of aspiration for many women.'

'Well, I don't know exactly what a pinnacle of aspiration is but it sounds jolly uncomfortable and I don't want to go anywhere near it.' Her hands shaking, Izzy stooped and pulled on her wedges. 'I can't believe you thought *you* were my goal. That's sick.'

'Izzy—'

'That would mean I'd targeted a total stranger for sex. There's a name for that.'

'Izzy!'

'What?' Powered by an attack of righteous indignation, Izzy stood straight, remembering that maintaining good posture was another of her medium-term goals. 'I don't have to listen to this. You ordered me to come here and I'm here. You told me to get out of the fountain and I did, even though I was actually having a *really* great time. So far I have obeyed your every command.' She wanted to stalk out but the ambition in her just wouldn't allow her to relinquish the opportunity. 'I could help backstage. I'll do anything. I'll scrub the stage. I'll clean the toilets. I'm not afraid of hard work. I just want to see what happens at a huge live event like that. *Please.*' She crossed her fingers behind her back, vowing to give money to charity and never swear again if he let her help.

He looked at her for a long moment and then shook his head. 'I don't need you causing trouble backstage.'

So that was that.

His phone rang and he glanced at her for a moment, as if deciding whether she could be trusted not to get into trouble while he answered it. 'Wait there…' His eyes still on her face, he took the call. '…Yes, I've listened to it. It's not the right sound.… I have no idea but they have forty-eight hours to come up with something else.…'

Eavesdropping madly, Izzy wondered what wasn't 'the right sound.' Needing to look at something other than him, her eyes wandered around his office and she saw a series of black-and-white photographs of various artists, all legends in the music industry. Musicians she'd grown up admiring. *People he knew personally.*

She wondered if they had fought the same uphill battle to be heard.

Had people told them to give up and get a proper job?

Had they been ridiculed and ignored?

When he finally put the phone down she gestured to the photographs. 'You have friends in high places.'

'Unfortunately none of them seem to be able to come up with the right song for the charity single.'

She'd intended to get out of his office as fast as possible, but suddenly her feet were glued to the floor. 'What sort of song are you looking for?' The words tumbled out from her mouth and she could see from his exasperated expression that she'd sounded like a desperate, breathless groupie. 'It's just that I could help you with that.'

His expression said everything she needed to know about his opinion of her musical talent. 'You just don't give up, do you?'

'No, I don't. And if I were a man, people would praise my tenacity, but ambition isn't seen as an attractive trait in a woman for some reason.' Reeling from yet another blow to her confidence,

Izzy stalked towards the door. 'Forget it. I'll see myself out.'

'Do *not* leave this room when we're talking. And this has nothing to do with your gender. You cannot deny that your last record bombed.'

First a blow then a punch. For a moment Izzy couldn't breathe. 'No, I can't deny that. Thanks for reminding me, because if someone doesn't throw that at me occasionally I get so full of myself I can't fit my enormous ego through the door. You're absolutely right. It bombed. In fact, I'd go so far as to say it was a spectacular failure. And now we've finally agreed on something, I'll leave you to get back to work.'

'I am trying to find a record that will be a huge commercial success.'

'And what would someone like me know about choosing a commercial success, is that what you're saying?' The humiliation and sheer sense of failure never left her, but it also drove her forward. Part of her wanted to tell him that it hadn't actually been *her* record but what was the point of that? She'd sung it, hadn't she? People didn't listen to a song and think 'Well, she obviously didn't write that so it isn't her fault it sucks.' They either liked a song or they didn't. As far as they were concerned it was her song. They didn't think about where the song came from.

And that record had taught her the second most important lesson of her life....

That if her chance ever came again, she'd sing nothing she hadn't written herself and nothing that she didn't love.

If she bombed again then she'd only have herself to blame.

But clearly getting another chance to bomb wasn't going to be easy.

Pride held her smile in place as she pulled open the door. 'I'm obviously as much use to you as a swimming pool without water so I'll let you get on with your day.'

'Wait!' His voice thundered through the open doorway and she saw Serena's eyes widen in surprise as she glanced up from her desk in the reception area.

So clearly he didn't usually speak to people like that, Izzy thought blankly.

Just her.

She was about to walk through the door when it slammed shut in front of her nose. Six foot four of muscular angry male stood between her and the exit.

'You don't just walk out when I'm talking to you.'

'I do when I don't like what I'm hearing.' Anger mingled with a much more dangerous emotion. This close she could feel the power pulsing from him, almost taste the lethal flash of his temper. Resisting the terrifying explosion of excitement that came from being this close to him, she tried to walk past him. 'Excuse me.'

'Where are you going? You don't know your way around.'

'I'll find my own way.' She hated the fact that there was a lump in her throat. Hated the fact that she'd let him get to her.

'I cleared an hour this afternoon to give you a tour of the grounds. I'll do it now.'

Not an apology. No 'I'm sorry if I was rude.' No 'Let's hear you sing then' or 'Prove me wrong, Izzy.'

A tour of the grounds.

'Save it for the coach parties.'

'You need to know what's off limits.'

She gave a humourless laugh, horrified to discover that the sound was almost a sob.

She needed to get out of here.

'I think I know what's off limits, Your Highness.' She risked a glance and then wished she hadn't because even a brief glimpse of those moody, sensual features was enough to throw her off balance. 'I can find my own way around and I'd hate you to waste another minute of your working day having to nursemaid someone like me.'

Someone like me.

If that song hadn't already been written, she would have written it.

Except that no one would have wanted to listen.

Pushing past him, she stalked out of his office and slammed the door behind her.

She'd targeted him because of his role in the music industry.

Not because she'd seen herself as a future princess.

Adapting speedily to that shift in his perceptions of her, Matteo strode after her and eventually caught up with her as she stalked across the courtyard and into the English rose garden.

It didn't need a glance at those stiff shoulders to know that he'd hurt her feelings badly and he cursed himself for his lack of tact, because the last thing he needed was an upset woman on his hands. Along with everything else, he didn't have time to handle female tantrums. Even on such short acquaintance he knew her well enough to know she wouldn't hesitate to walk out and he couldn't allow that to happen. He couldn't allow anything to detract from his brother's engagement.

He needed Izzy to stay here.

Which presented him with a dilemma. In order to keep her happy was he supposed to lie? Tell her that she had a great voice and that she was going to be the 'next big thing'?

Apart from the obvious fact that there was no useful role someone like her could play in planning the final details of the concert, he knew just how many popstar wannabes had wasted their lives hoping they'd make it big, only to remain in obscurity forever.

Exasperation shot through him. He could never understand why the millions of talentless hopefuls couldn't hear the difference between their own voices and those of true singers. Even if their mothers heaped on false praise, surely they'd listened to themselves? Were they deaf?

'Izzy, wait!'

Her hair swung with each angry stride and she didn't pause.

'I said *wait*.' He thundered the order, injecting

his tone with an authority that would have had his staff jumping. Unfortunately for him Izzy was made of sterner stuff. She carried on walking, her espadrilles crunching on the gravel path until his hand closed on her shoulder. 'I'm not accustomed to having to chase guests round the palazzo.'

'But I'm not a guest, am I?' She shrugged him off. 'Let's drop the pretence. You can't stand the sight of me, which is fine because I can't stand being here. If I'm here for more than a day I'm going to suffocate in this formal atmosphere.'

'*Maledizione*, will you stand still and listen when I talk to you!' Opting for his last resort, he caught her arm and spun her back towards him but the movement knocked her off balance and her body flattened against his. The flare of attraction was immediate and fierce and Matteo sucked in a breath and released her instantly.

Blue eyes blazed into his. 'Yes, that's right, Your Highness, we're jolly well going to ignore that too, because I don't want to find you attractive any more than you want to find me attractive.'

She was the most aggravating, infuriating woman he'd met.

Ballsy one minute, insecure the next.

But always sexy.

And it was the most disturbing level of sexy he'd ever encountered. It was precisely because of the chemistry that he knew any relationship between them was absolutely out of the question. He never allowed his libido to compromise his judgement and yet with Izzy he found himself right on the edge of control. Not wanting to dwell on the fact that he'd slipped over that edge at least once, he swiftly changed the subject. 'You're angry because I don't want you helping out with the concert, but frankly I have no idea what you could do to help. It's the biggest live event of the concert calendar. And you're—'

'I'm what? *I'm what, Your Highness?*' Those eyes darkened like the sky before a thunderstorm. 'I'm just a manufactured pop singer? How would you know what I am? You were in such a hurry to separate me from that microphone last night you didn't bother to listen to me singing. Say anything you like about me, but don't tell me my voice is bad because I *know* that isn't true.'

Confronted by that degree of conviction, Matteo proceeded with the caution of a man treading onto very, *very* thin ice. 'I watched a few episodes of *Singing Star.*'

That statement was greeted by silence.

He watched as the flush spread over her pretty face and waited for her to explode in a defensive tirade, but instead she flushed scarlet and wrapped her arms around herself.

'Oh, well, in that case I probably can't blame you for not rating me. It was rubbish. *Seriously* crap.'

Thrown by that unexpectedly honest response, Matteo was forced to acknowledge that Izzy Jackson continually surprised him. 'That sort of show isn't there to showcase musical talent. It's there to make money.'

'I happen to agree. But that doesn't mean that no one who appears on the show has anything to offer. There are all sorts of reasons why a person goes on a show like that.'

'What were yours?'

The silence stretched on and on while the sun beat down on them. Given that she was a talker, her lack of response was all the more marked. He'd seen wicked Izzy, flirty Izzy and cheeky Izzy, but there was something about vulnerable Izzy that tugged at him deep inside.

Her slim shoulders lifted. 'What difference does it make?'

'You must have decided to go on the show for a reason.'

'I'm an incurable exhibitionist as you've pointed out. Why perform to a hundred people if you can perform to several million?' Her response was flippant and transparently not reflective of the truth but Matteo resisted the urge to dig deeper.

What did it matter what her reasons were for appearing on that awful show? The less he knew about her, the better. The less time he spent with her, the better.

In fact, he should leave her right now and get back to work instead of standing here noticing that she'd caught the sun on her face.

It was obvious she didn't expect him to nurse-maid her so there was no reason for him to hang around. She could occupy herself without him.

His eyes slid to the tempting curve of her mouth and he felt that same explosion of sensation that had tormented him the night before. His brain was telling him one thing and his body another. 'I'll show you round.' His hard tone reflected his own inner conflict. 'And you'd better wear sunscreen. You're English. You're not used to the heat.'

Her eyes lifted to his and he knew she was thinking what he was thinking. That nothing the sun produced was as powerful as the heat they generated between them.

'I thought you were snowed under with work.'

Battling an inexplicable urge to kiss her, Matteo took a step back. 'That doesn't mean I intend to neglect my duties as host.'

'Host?' She laughed. 'You mean host as in "keep an eye on Izzy" duty, don't you? I think you've done enough of that for one week. Or maybe you mean "host" as in the sort that gives a home to a parasite. That's how you see me, isn't it? A user.'

He wasn't sure how he saw her. He couldn't see clearly through the fog of sexual tension that pressed in on them. 'You were the one who told me I was your goal, so if there was a misunderstanding then you are to blame. And picking a fight is not going to make this any easier.' He noticed that her hair had dried curly. It tumbled over her shoulders in unrestrained wildness and he had a vivid memory of the way those silky soft waves had felt against his skin. 'We'll start with the swimming pool as you seem to like water so much.'

'Fine—' she gave him an odd look '—if that's what you want then lead on. Give me the guided tour, complete with commentary. Show me the official swimming pool, although I still think the unofficial one is more fun. And if there was a misunderstanding it was because it didn't cross my mind that you'd think my goal was anything other than professional. Do women seriously do that? Target you for marriage?'

'Yes.' Trying to block out the memory of her twirling in his fountain wearing nothing but a bright fuchsia bikini, Matteo strode through the rose garden and took the steps that led to the pool.

'So women target you just because you're a prince. That's weird. Oh—' she stopped next to him and stared at the pool with the stunning sea views beyond '—this is gorgeous. OK, maybe it's not so weird. If I married you I could look at this all day.' She grinned and punched his arm gently. 'Just kidding by the way. Do you realise that you turn pale when people mention marriage?'

Matteo breathed deeply. 'There are changing rooms through that door.'

'Or I could just strip off here.' Her hands dropped to the zip of her shorts and then she burst out laughing. 'I wish you could see your face. You *really* need to chill, Your Highness. Is this just because of the concert or are you always this uptight?'

'I am not uptight.' He spoke through his teeth and she gave him a sympathetic look.

'It might help if you took off that suit. It's too hot for that.'

'I had meetings this morning.'

'Until I dragged you away from them. I like it here. It's peaceful. To be honest I wasn't sure I'd like "peaceful" because I'm used to something different, but I do.' Stooping, she fished out a leaf that had fallen onto the surface of the pool, the movement exposing even more of her long, slim legs. And there, high on her thigh, was a tiny tattoo in the shape of a butterfly. 'Let's call a truce because frankly all this conflict is messing with my concentration.'

His own concentration was shot to pieces so it should have been a welcome suggestion but he couldn't stop looking at that butterfly. 'Truce?'

'Yes.' She straightened and brushed her hair out of her eyes. 'You get on with your work, I'll get on with mine.'

'Five minutes ago you were deeply offended.'

She shrugged. 'I'm resilient. One of the advantages of being crushed a lot is that you become very experienced at bouncing back. Of course it's a blow that you won't let me help but I never bear grudges. Life's too short. So are we cool?'

Matteo had never felt hotter in his life and it made no sense. He spent plenty of time with exceptionally beautiful women whose daily focus was grooming—so how could a pair of frayed denim shorts and one single tattoo have such an inflammatory effect on his libido?

Blue eyes twinkled into his. 'Are you OK? Say something. Preferably something nice and not "Izzy, your voice is crap." That way we'll maintain this lovely harmonious atmosphere.'

It was her mouth, he decided. Yes, her hair was wild and her clothes casual, but her mouth was a work of art. An almost perfect curve announcing her sexuality and he had a clear memory of the way that mouth had felt under his.

Matteo couldn't remember the last time he'd had to fight his own impulses and he knew she was fighting the same impulse from the way she suddenly frowned and looked away from him.

But eye contact wasn't necessary to fuel chemistry this intense. It had a life of its own and the heat scorched both of them, burning up willpower and good intentions.

'Um, this is awkward.' She drew in an unsteady

breath, watching as a tiny bird skimmed water from the still surface of the pool. 'So let's just talk about it and get it out of the way. You're thinking about that kiss. So am I. But you kissed me because you were angry with me, no other reason. I drove you a little crazy.' Delving into the pocket of her shorts she pulled out a pair of sunglasses and slipped them onto her nose. 'We'd both been drinking. End of story.'

But *he'd* drunk virtually nothing and the absence of an excuse made his behaviour all the more disturbing.

Her expression was hidden by the glasses. 'Let's just finish this tour so you can get back to work. How do I get down to the beach? I'm more of a sea girl than a pool girl.'

And now he'd seen her in the fountain it was all too easy to imagine her in the sea, those long limbs kicking gracefully through the water. And from there it was a small step to imagining those same long limbs wrapped around his waist.

Matteo undid the top button of his shirt. 'There's only one path and it's very steep. You need to be careful not to go close to the edge of the cliffs or you could fall. I'll show you.' Striding ahead of her so that she was out of his field of vision, he led her down a set of stone steps and back onto the sweep of grass that led from the palazzo to the cliffs.

'So that amphitheatre place where you hold the concert—is it near here?' Once again she'd taken off her espadrilles and this time they dangled from her fingers as she walked across the grass, as light on her feet as a ballerina.

'It's about an hour south of here.' He dragged his gaze from her bright pink toenails. 'You seem to carry your shoes more than you wear them.'

'That's because I fall in love with pretty shoes and then discover I can't walk in them. I watched the concert on TV last year. Incredible.' She stretched out her arms and lifted her face to the sun. 'I suppose it's useless to ask if you can get me a ticket? Given that you won't let me help, at least you could let me watch. I could hover backstage.'

The last thing he wanted was Izzy backstage, distracting him with her soft mouth and her laughing eyes. 'You'll be back in England before the concert.'

'I suppose you don't trust me not to grab the microphone. So how did you get involved in the music industry anyway? I mean, it isn't exactly a normal focus for a prince.' She stooped to pick a daisy from the grass, the movement once again bringing that tempting tattoo into his line of vision.

Matteo felt as if he was being suffocated. 'I had friends in the music industry. Some of us decided it would be fun to raise money through a rock concert.'

'So you get to enjoy yourself and raise money at the same time. Smart move.' She threaded the head of the daisy through the stalk of another. 'The concert has some really high-profile sponsors. You have powerful friends, Your Highness. I suppose you speak a million languages?'

'Didn't you discover the answer to that when you did your "research" on me?' Matteo found himself fascinated by the dexterity of those slim fingers as she skilfully wove herself a daisy chain. And somehow his brain managed to move from daisy chains to something altogether less innocent.

'I found out that you have a shockingly high IQ.' Her voice was matter-of-fact. 'And that you joined the air force. You flew fast jets until the palace decided it was too dangerous and you had to switch to helicopters. That must have been difficult for you.'

'Did your research tell you that?'

'No need to be snappy, especially when someone is being sympathetic.' She tilted her wrist so that the delicate daisy chain slid to the right place on her arm. 'Being forced to give up something you are burning to do can sometimes feel like not breathing.'

It had felt exactly like that but Matteo had no intention of discussing anything that personal with anyone, let alone her.

Undaunted by his lack of response, she glanced at him. 'So why did you give up flying helicopters?'

That was a more comfortable question to answer. 'I had a heavy workload of official engagements. That became my priority.'

'Because your brother was too busy pursuing his own business interests to do his share.'

Matteo's eyes narrowed. 'Just how in depth *was* this research of yours?'

'If we'd got as far as a conversation I wanted to be prepared. I wanted to understand you. So while he was off doing his own thing, you were covering for him. And last night, you were protective of him…. Hmm…' Twisting a daisy between her fingers, she glanced at him thoughtfully. 'So I'm guessing you're just relieved not to be the eldest and have all that rule-the-world stuff ahead of you. You have powerful ideals and a strong sense of duty but you don't want all the pomp and attention that goes with being Crown Prince. That's why you like it here. You can fulfil the role expected of you, but still live by your own rules.'

Astounded by the depth of her perception, Matteo lifted his eyebrows. 'You discovered all that from a search engine?'

'I filled in the blanks.'

And she'd filled them in with astonishing accuracy. 'Wealth and privilege come with responsibility. I have always understood that.' It wasn't true, of course. He hadn't always understood that. It had taken a brutal lesson for him to really see the obligation that came with his role.

'People have expectations of you. It's a bit like running a business, I suppose.' She picked another daisy and started another chain. 'Royalty, Inc. or Monarchy.com. So that would make your dad sort of the CEO, right?'

It took Matteo a moment to work out who she was talking about because he'd never before heard his father referred to as 'Dad.'

'I suppose so.' He marvelled that she took such

pleasure in something as simple as making a daisy chain.

'And it would make the public your customers.' With a pleased smile she slipped the second daisy chain onto her other wrist and admired it.

'I suppose so.'

'And right now you have unhappy customers. There are grumblings about you being detached from the real world and that's why you're all so hyped up about this engagement.' She glanced at him briefly. 'The scandalous Jacksons wouldn't be your ideal pick, but you're hoping Allegra will be the bridge between your family and the public.'

'This was Alex's choice—'

'But your parents are allowing it because they think it might help the reputation of Monarchy, Inc.' She stuck out her wrist and smiled at her bracelet. 'Cute, isn't it? I haven't done that since I was about six. Shame it has to die.'

Normally he found this part of the grounds restful and tranquil but today there was a dangerous tension in the air. A tension not helped by those tiny shorts. Never had an item of clothing been so well named.

'I need to get back to work. From now on I'd

like you to tell someone where you're going when you leave the palazzo.'

'I'm supposed to file a route every time I leave the house? What if I don't know where I'm going until I get there? This place is *huge*. Exploring will be fun.' She squinted across the grass towards the cliffs. 'So what's that white building? You haven't shown me that.'

'It's my recording studio.'

He saw her face change. Saw the moment that she sensed opportunity, like a hound on the trail of a fox.

'You actually have a recording studio in your grounds?' She virtually salivated, her eyes hungry and hopeful at the same time. 'A real one? With a vocal booth and everything?'

'It's out of bounds.'

'Can I see it?' She almost shimmered with excitement and Matteo decided that if he didn't show her she was likely to break in anyway.

'It houses millions of pounds worth of equipment.'

'I want to see it, not steal it.' She was already sprinting across the grass and Matteo was forced to lengthen his stride to keep up with her. Pausing by the door she almost quivered with anticipation as he pulled out the key.

'I can't believe you have your own recording studio.'

He opened the door and heard her gasp as she saw the glass-fronted control room.

'I've died and gone to heaven—if I'd known you had this here I would have kidnapped you and held you to ransom. Why didn't my research tell me you had this?'

'Next door is a small theatre with some instruments. There's a great deal of expensive equipment here which is why we keep it locked.' His phone rang. Given the state of his arousal he should have been relieved by the interruption but instead he felt a flash of irritation. Seeing that it was his father, he took the call and Izzy made straight for the piano like an iron filing to a magnet.

Listening to his father's warning that Isabelle Jackson was trouble, Matteo watched her as she stroked one of the keys with the tip of her finger. All she was doing was touching his piano and yet even that movement was sensual.

His father was still talking.

'I've read about her. She'll try and use you if she can. Exploit the connection—'

Izzy's head lifted and their eyes met. One look at her expression told him that his father had spoken loudly enough for her to hear his comment that had, unfortunately, been expressed in English. He switched to Italian. 'That isn't going to happen.'

Did his father really think the lesson hadn't been learned?

Without realising he was doing it, Matteo flexed his damaged hand and when he terminated the call, Izzy was still watching him.

'Just as a matter of interest, does he mean sexually or professionally?' Her voice casual, she fiddled with the keys of the piano. 'Because in the interests of full disclosure I ought to tell you that I'm not interested in you sexually because it would mess with my head, but I'd use you professionally in a heartbeat if you'd let me.'

Heat spread through his body. 'You overheard.'

'Of course. Kings obviously don't feel the need to speak in hushed voices.'

Matteo drew in a long breath. 'My father is concerned about anything that might affect the monarchy.'

'And one Jackson in the family is enough for anyone.' Her fingers slid seductively over the keys of the piano. 'So rock stars come here to record in peace and quiet.' Her hair tumbled forward, obscuring her features so that it was impossible for him to read her expression.

He didn't know if she was hurt, offended or angry.

And Matteo didn't know how he felt either. All he knew was that the air in the studio felt thicker and heavier than usual. Oppressive. 'Yes, rock stars come here. We have producers and sound engineers. Everything they need. It's state of the art.' *So was her mouth.* And the slope of her shoulders and the smoothness of her skin. And the way those long, smooth legs went on for ever.

He wondered if her parents knew about her tattoo.

'Could I stay here for a while? I'd really like to play the piano.'

Matteo was still listing reasons why he shouldn't touch her. 'You play?'

'No, I just thought I'd vandalize it. Yes, I play.' This time there was a dangerous snap in her tone and when she lifted her head to look at him it was matched by the flash in her eyes. 'Do you even realise how patronising you sound sometimes?'

The room was soundproofed and windowless and as a result there was nothing to distract from the woman—from the subtle floral scent of her perfume that wove itself around his senses and slowly drove him mad. The powerful explosion of awareness confirmed what he already knew—that sexual attraction was no respecter of boundaries.

His phone rang again but this time he ignored it. 'I am *not* patronising you, but this place is not a playground. It's designed for serious musicians.'

'Ah, and I'm not serious, of course. I'm a joke. A national laughingstock.' Her tone was brittle, the cheerful smile gone from her pretty face. She stood abruptly and Matteo breathed deeply, telling himself that honesty was kinder in the long run.

'All I'm saying is—'

'I know exactly what you're saying. If you'll excuse me I'll find my own way back. Five more minutes with you and I won't have any confidence left to lose.' Snatching up her shoes, she stalked past him, her bare feet soundless on the floor. 'And you can reassure your father that if I want something I am always up front about it. I asked you straight out if I could help with Rock 'n' Royal. I call that asking for what you want, but if you want to call that "using" then go ahead. Thanks for the tour. It was really illuminating.'

She yanked open the door and immediately the breeze from the sea lifted and flirted with her hair.

Matteo could have smoothed the situation easily. He had the skills. But he didn't use them. He didn't want things smooth. He didn't want to encourage that chemistry. Nor was he prepared to give false flattery. No one, not even her own parents, who should surely be her biggest supporters, could describe her as a serious musician.

And surely no one who put themselves up for public scrutiny in a show like *Singing Star* could still be sensitive. The show had been slated. *She'd* been slated.

And if she was offended and kept her distance from him, that would be a good thing.

Having rationalised his behaviour, he watched as she tugged on her shoes. 'Dinner is at eight.'

She didn't look at him. 'I'll eat in my room. Isn't that what usually happens to prisoners?' With that parting shot she stalked off towards the palazzo, leaving Matteo staring after her.

CHAPTER FIVE

MISERABLE, angry and totally humiliated, Izzy pulled on her pyjamas and curled up on her bed. It was all very well believing in yourself but what was the point in believing in yourself if everyone else just put you down?

Perhaps everyone was right. Her voice was rubbish, she had no talent and no one was ever going to take her seriously. She was kidding herself if she thought anything was ever going to change. There was perseverance and then there was being just plain deluded.

Perhaps she should follow Allegra's advice, get a proper job and forget her dream.

Look at me, I'm not what you see...

Deep inside there's part of me, longing to break free...

The song just wouldn't leave her alone and she sat up and rubbed the tears from her cheeks, furious with herself for being so pathetic.

If she gave up she was definitely going to fail,

wasn't she? No one who gave up had ever succeeded, but sometimes people who had failed
loads of times eventually made it. Just because
you didn't succeed the first time or the tenth,
didn't mean you wouldn't on the hundredth.

Desperate for human comfort, she toyed with
her phone.

She could ring her mother, but what would be
the point of that? All she'd get was a bracing lec-
ture on getting back up when life knocks you
over when what she really wanted was a hug.
And the yearning for a hug surprised her because
Chantelle had never been tactile and Izzy had
given up hoping or even wishing for a closer relationship. What chance was there of that when
she wasn't even allowed to call her 'Mum'? It had
to be 'Chantelle,' as if the use of her first name
would somehow roll back the years.

Deciding that there was no lonelier feeling than
looking at a phone full of contacts, none of whom
you could call, Izzy flung her phone back in her
bag.

Suddenly she was a young child again, sitting
on her bottom in the dirt, crying and reaching out
her arms to her mother—a mother who stayed at

a distance and watched impatiently as her child struggled.

'If I pick you up, Izzy, you'll never learn to get up by yourself. Stop crying and stand up.'

Once in a while, Izzy thought miserably, it would be nice to at least have someone hold out a hand to help her up.

She thought about texting Allegra but then remembered that she wasn't supposed to use her phone. And anyway, Allegra was probably still basking in the ecstasy of being engaged to a prince and Izzy didn't want to ruin that.

There was no one she could talk to and the truth was there was no point. People didn't understand her love of music, they never had and the fact that no one understood her was infinitely depressing.

Despite what people thought, it wasn't about the attention. She didn't sing because she wanted an audience. She sang because she *had* to sing. There was something inside her that made it impossible not to sing. Since she was tiny, she'd had tunes and words in her head. It had driven Chantelle crazy that she was always singing, but Izzy could no more stop singing than she could stop breathing. It was part of who she was.

And right now she didn't like that part one little bit.

She almost wished she *could* give up so that she could stop being crushed by disappointment at regular intervals.

But of all the rejections she'd received in her life nothing had been quite so crushing as the prince's total dismissal of her talent. Or maybe it just mattered more because it was him.

Izzy slid off the bed and wandered through to the luxurious bathroom. She removed her streaked make-up, splashed her face with cold water and looked in the mirror.

Her eyes were red, and without make-up her face was almost ethereally pale.

She looked a million miles from the successful singer she wanted to be.

Staring at her reflection she reminded herself that every journey was made up of single steps and no one was going to take those steps for you. She just needed to stay focused.

She was still stunned by the discovery that he had a recording studio in his home. Envy seeped through her. He could just walk into it at any time of the day and start playing. Drums, acoustic guitar, piano—

Her palms itched with the need to play. The piano was amazing. If only he'd given her permission to use it, she'd be as happy as a monkey in a banana plantation.

Walking over to the window, Izzy stared wistfully across the floodlit grounds towards the recording studio. Her eyes narrowed thoughtfully.

The piano was in the outer room. She didn't even need to go into the rooms that housed all the expensive equipment. All she needed to do was get through the first door.

Her heart started to beat faster.

A slow smile spread across her face.

She wondered if Matteo had realised that he hadn't locked the door behind him when he'd left.

Matteo lay sprawled on the sofa in his office as he listened to the final track.

Was he being too fussy?

That last song was fine. Nothing special, but not awful.

With a curse he reached for the bottle of beer on the table next to him.

He didn't want 'fine.' He wanted mesmerising. He wanted emotional, heartbreaking, beautiful—

a song everyone would be humming and words that would embed themselves into people's brains.

He couldn't even put his finger on exactly what was wrong, except that everything he'd heard had been instantly forgettable and he wanted unforgettable. He wanted it to touch hearts.

Touch hearts? Laughing silently at himself, he finished the beer.

Who was he kidding?

He wanted the song to raise money. Piles of the stuff. He wanted the song to be so damn good the whole world downloaded it. He wanted the music websites to crash but nothing he'd heard had the emotion needed to guarantee the song would be a global success.

Pulling his phone out of his pocket, Matteo tapped out a quick email.

They were running out of time and options. And as if the concert wasn't enough to give him a headache, he now had Izzy Jackson to think about.

His jaw tightened as he contemplated what the hell he was going to do with her.

As she'd threatened, she hadn't turned up to dinner and he'd been too busy with his guests to chase her down.

Or perhaps he hadn't wanted to chase her down.

Restless, his mind uncomfortably preoccupied with the past, he rose to his feet and strolled over to the tall windows that overlooked the landscaped gardens. The lake was floodlit, but beyond that everything was in darkness.

Or at least, it was supposed to be in darkness.

Matteo stared in the direction of the recording studio.

Was it his imagination or had he seen a flicker of light?

No. The place was locked, and—

He gave a faint groan. *He'd forgotten to lock it.* He'd been so busy trying not to grab her that he'd forgotten to lock the door. And she would have noticed that, of course, because Izzy Jackson didn't miss a thing. Not if it might help her achieve one of her goals.

Anger erupted inside him and the anger felt good because it blew away the more uncomfortable thoughts that had seriously disturbed his evening. Nursing that anger like a vulnerable flame, he strode out of the door.

He'd *told* her the place was out of bounds. With well over a million pounds worth of recording equipment in the studio, not to mention the musical instruments, it wasn't a place for someone inexperienced. She was irresponsible, aggravating—

His mouth tight, tension mounting with every angry stride, Matteo reached the recording studio in record time. A summer storm was brewing and he could hear the wild crash of waves exploding over rocks at the foot of the cliffs, but nothing that nature produced could match the force of his own temper.

As far as he was concerned this was the final straw.

She had no respect for rules. No concept of appropriate behaviour.

He'd told her the place was out of bounds but she didn't listen to the word *no* unless it suited her.

Enveloped by the darkness, he opened the door, ready to unleash hell.

And then stopped.

A clear sweet voice resonated around the studio, the quality and emotion enough to wipe his mind of all thoughts except one—

This was the song he'd been waiting for.

He'd entered the studio ready to let rip, but now he could do nothing but listen as her voice soared and her fingers flew over the keys creating harmonies that made him catch his breath.

Emotional, heartbreaking, beautiful—the song was all those things and more and he was knocked sideways by the beauty of the sound. She was mesmerizing and there was a musical sophistication in her performance that outstripped anything he'd played over the past few months.

Goose bumps spread across his skin and then she hit a top note and those goose bumps changed to chills. She wasn't just good, she was incredible, and he was afraid to breathe in case he drew attention to himself and disturbed the flow of the music.

She reminded him of one of the Sirens from Greek mythology, the sound she made a dangerous enchantment luring enamoured sailors to their deaths.

But this time she wasn't singing for anyone else.

She was singing for herself. In the dark, where he couldn't be distracted by a vibrant sequined dress, red lips or towering stilettos. Here, in the dark loneliness of the empty recording studio, there was just the woman and the voice, and the voice was world class.

The rich, perfect sound lifted the tiny hairs on

the back of his neck and sent sensation pouring through his body, rapidly followed by a stinging infusion of guilt as he realised how wrong he'd been about her.

He'd called her talentless.

Opportunistic.

Slowly confronting the magnitude of his error, Matteo listened to the words of the song—a soulful lament urging people not to judge from the outside.

Look at me, I'm not what you see...

The lyrics were uncomfortably apt and he stirred under the weight of remorse because, although it was true her image had projected something different, he was a man who prided himself on being able to see beneath the surface of every person and every situation. But with her he'd been blind. He'd seen the press coverage, the sequined dress and he'd judged, but he hadn't listened.

The harmony and chord progression were skilled and unusual, but what really stunned him was the rare purity of her voice. She was insanely good, her talent so glaringly obvious that he, who had heard just about everything in his years listening to music, was speechless.

Had she sung like that at his brother's engagement party?

He yanked his mind back, forcing himself to remember the moment she'd grabbed the microphone. What little he remembered was nothing like that. Her voice had been hard and a little forced. False. Desperate.

Look at me, I'm not what you see...

She could have been singing the song for him. If it hadn't been for the fact she hadn't realised he was in the room he would have thought she'd picked it especially to make her point because it was an honest reflection of his own attitude to her.

He didn't recognise the song and although he couldn't see her face he knew from the depth of emotion she poured into the sound that her cheeks would be wet with tears as she hit the last few bars and sang, *'That's not who I am...'*

Silence followed.

Matteo was about to declare himself when she sensed him. Or maybe he made a noise. Either way, her head whipped round.

'Hello? Is someone—?' She must have made out his outline in the semi-darkness because she gave a soft gasp of fright. 'What are you doing here? It's the middle of the night.'

'I could ask you the same question.' He flicked on the light and saw her flinch away from the beam and wrap her arms around herself.

'Switch that off!'

She was in her pyjamas. A soft shade of pink and covered in...*frogs*?

She looked impossibly young—far too young to have produced such a rich, perfect sound. If he hadn't heard it himself, he wouldn't have believed it.

For a moment they both stared at each other.

He noticed that even without the make-up her lashes were long and thick, providing a startling contrast to those spectacular blue eyes. She had a sweet face, he thought. Pretty, rather than beautiful.

'Stop staring!' Visibly self-conscious, she gave him a furious look and hunched her shoulders.

The air was thick with sexual tension and it exasperated him because right now he didn't want to think about the intensity of the chemistry. He didn't want to *feel* that because although he'd been wrong to call her talentless he hadn't been wrong to call her an opportunist.

'You often play the piano in your pyjamas?'

'*Obviously* I wasn't expecting you to be stalk-ing me.' Tense as a bow, she pushed her hair out of her eyes in an entirely feminine gesture that told him she would rather have walked on needles than let him see her without her make-up.

He could have told her that the make-up made no difference to the attraction. If anything, his struggle was all the greater for seeing her because he now had a disturbingly clear idea of how she'd look first thing in the morning emerging from sex-induced sleep.

Her cheeks pink, she stood abruptly, but he noticed that she carefully closed the lid of the piano, protecting the keys. 'Go ahead, yell at me. I know I shouldn't have come in here but I honestly wasn't doing any harm and I didn't think you'd even catch me. Are you having me followed or something?'

'I was working. I saw the light go on.'

'You were working at two in the morning?' Without looking at him, she gathered up a stack of papers she'd piled on the piano stool next to her. 'You need a different job. From where I'm sitting, yours sucks.'

'It has its moments. Like five minutes ago when I heard that song. Who wrote it?'

Her spine was a rigid line. 'Why do you care?'

'Because it's incredible. Because I haven't heard it before. Because I want whoever wrote it to write something for me.' Fascinated by the feminine curves outlined by the flimsy pyjamas, Matteo struggled valiantly to keep his mind on the music. 'Do you have a contact number for him?'

'You're *so* sexist.'

'Her then.' Impatient for an answer and desperate to remove himself from this sexually charged atmosphere, Matteo retrieved his phone. 'Name? Number?'

'This songwriter doesn't write songs for other people.'

'They wrote that for you?'

'You think I stole it?' Her voice had a brittle edge to it. 'Thanks.'

It was a physical effort not to haul her against him and kiss her again as he had on that first night. For some reason her nude lips were every bit as appealing as the glossy, strawberry-red version. He knew they'd be soft because he'd already kissed her. He knew she'd taste sweet, because he'd already tasted her.

And although part of him wanted to tell her that he thought her voice was sensational, he knew that offering up that degree of praise would shift the nature of their relationship. Experience told him that the only thing keeping them apart was the thin layer of animosity they'd managed to construct. A layer that was now torn and full of holes.

Matteo struggled to draw together the flimsy, ragged edges of the protection he'd spun. 'I didn't know you played the piano.'

'Yes, well, I think we've already established that there are a lot of things you don't know, including when to relax and have fun.' She stuffed the papers into an oversize bag and dragged it onto her shoulder. As usual her feet were bare and this time she didn't seem to have bothered even to carry her shoes.

Matteo breathed deeply, trying to find the balance between antagonising her further and crossing the barriers he'd erected. 'I'll overlook the fact that you broke into my recording studio if you give me the phone number of the songwriter.'

'I didn't break in. I walked in. You left the door unlocked.' Chin in the air, she marched past him but he caught her arm, spinning her around to face him.

'*Maledizione,* Izzy, *who* wrote the song?'

Finally she looked at him. Straight at him.

For a moment he thought he saw a sheen of tears glaze her eyes. Then she blinked.

'*I* did. I wrote the song.' And before he had time to react she twisted her arm from his grip and vanished out of the door.

Arrogant, judgemental, annoying—boiling with fury, Izzy sprinted back over the grass towards the palazzo, grateful for the dark. So much for lifting her mood by singing. Not only had a man she lusted after more than she'd ever lusted after a man before seen her looking her worst, she'd completely embarrassed herself.

The irony of it made her want to scream.

She'd planned every second of her performance at the engagement party in an attempt to gain his attention. She'd chosen her red sequin dress with care. She'd spent *hours* on her make-up. And he'd finally listened when she was dressed in her pyjamas, barefaced and singing to herself in the dark. She'd spent her life on the lookout for opportunities, and when one had finally come she hadn't been ready for it.

Furious with herself and not exactly understanding why, Izzy carried on running until she reached the side door of the palazzo. She sprinted up the elegant curving staircase to her turret bedroom and slammed the door shut.

It opened immediately and Matteo strode into the room without knocking.

Izzy turned like a cornered animal.

'Get out of here.'

He ignored her and slammed the door shut just as she had. Only he was on the inside. And she was still in her pyjamas, her heart pounding.

'You don't want to come near me right now because frankly I am so angry with you I might hit you!'

He planted his legs firmly apart, the stance telling her that he wasn't budging. 'You wrote that song? Is that the truth?'

'Do I get thrown in the dungeons if I punch you?'

He didn't smile. 'I can't believe you wrote it.'

'Because I'm a talentless loser?' Feeling naked and exposed, Izzy wanted to grab a cardigan but she didn't want to give him the satisfaction of knowing just how much he unsettled her. And truthfully she wasn't sure a cardigan was going to solve the problem. The vulnerability she felt was beneath the surface.

'Because that song is incredible,' he said in a

thickened tone. 'And I did not at any point call you a loser.'

Izzy found it difficult to breathe.

He thought her song was incredible?

A strange buzzing feeling started in her head and suddenly she felt light-headed.

He thought her song was incredible.

The prince lifted an eyebrow. 'Are you going to say something?'

Izzy opened her mouth and closed it again without speaking.

He gave a sardonic smile. 'You go to extreme lengths to get me to hear you sing. If what you're telling me is the truth then you elbowed your way onto the stage with the precise intention of gaining my attention. And now you have my attention, you are mute?'

Izzy's mouth was dry. 'You really think my song is incredible?'

'Yes.'

The pounding turned to a rapid tattoo. As his words sank into her stunned brain, Izzy burst into tears.

Consternation flared in his eyes and he spread his hands in disbelief. 'Why are you crying? I am complimenting you.'

'That's why I'm crying,' Izzy sobbed, horrified by her loss of control but unable to stop it. 'No one ever compliments me. I'm not used to it.' Her breathing hiccoughed and she wiped her cheek on her shoulder. 'Sorry. Sorry. It's just…you don't understand how hard I've worked to get people to take me seriously—'

'I'm starting to get an idea.' His eyes gleamed dark with a mixture of disbelief and incredulity. 'You look a mess, Izzy Jackson.'

'Thanks.' She wiped her face with her palm. 'After the fiasco of *Singing Star* I didn't think I was going to get another chance. I sang badly on that stupid show, I know I did. And the song was rubbish. I should have refused to sing it but when you've waited ages for your big moment you don't go and blow it. Chantelle always told me to grab opportunities with both hands so that's sort of instinctive for me.'

He looked blank. 'Why do you call your mother "Chantelle"?'

'She prefers it.' Izzy pulled a tissue from her bag and blew her nose hard. '"Mum" makes her feel old. She's the one who drummed into me the need to seize opportunities. What she didn't tell me was that sometimes something that looks like an opportunity isn't.' It was hard enough to admit it to herself, let alone to someone like him. '*Singing Star* was just a big mistake, masquerading as an opportunity. I got it wrong and I'm paying for it because I will always be "that girl who sang that awful song on that awful reality show." That's all anyone sees now.'

'Not for much longer. So that song you were singing—*The Me You Don't See*—you wrote that because of what happened with the show?'

'No,' Izzy said honestly, 'I wrote it because of what happened with you.'

That got his attention. *'Me?'*

'At the party you took one look at me in my sequined dress and dragged me away from the microphone. You didn't even bother to listen.'

'Because that was not the time or the place to sing.'

'It was a party! It was the perfect time and place, but I was the wrong person because people took one look and judged.'

'Wait a minute—you say you wrote that song because of me. *When* did you write that song?'

'In the car on the way here.'

He was frowning. 'You didn't write anything while we were in the car.'

'I wrote it in my head. I was humming. You yelled at me to stop.'

'The humming was you writing the song? So how long did it take you to finish it?'

'I don't know.' No one had ever asked her that before. No one had shown that much interest. 'Fifteen minutes, I suppose? It just came in a rush. That's how it happens.'

'You've written other songs?'

'Millions. Well, maybe not *millions* exactly. But at least a hundred.'

'A hundred? You've written a hundred songs?' Incredulous eyes scanned her as if a fact like that should somehow have been visible. 'Have you ever played them to anyone?'

'I'm *always* trying to play them to people. Their response is always "Shut up, Izzy." So usually I just record them and store them on my computer—except when I occasionally try and take over the stage at royal engagement parties.' It was his eyes that made him so spectacular to look at, she decided. Dark, moody and full of secrets.

'And how long have you played the piano?' Suddenly he was firing questions at her and she found it unsettling because no one had ever shown such a degree of interest in her before. She was usually the one pushing herself forward while everyone ignored her.

'Since I was three. I played one at a friend's house and loved it so much I refused to move until my parents promised to buy one. They thought the craze would last about a week, but I loved it. I had to be dragged away from the piano to go to school. When I grew up I used it for composition and to accompany myself when I sing.' Izzy watched warily as he paced to the far side of her bedroom suite and stared into the darkness, his powerful shoulders a shield between her and the darkness. She couldn't help but imagine him without the shirt.

He turned suddenly and she coloured guiltily, hoping that he couldn't read her mind.

'I owe you an apology.' The words were dragged from him, but no matter how reluctantly expressed the apology was sweet. And unexpected. As unexpected as his lavish praise of her song.

Given that she didn't want to feel the way she was feeling about him, she decided it would do no harm to reinforce his bad side.

'Too right, you do. First you drag me from the stage and then you incarcerate me here and you've been generally mean—'

'I'm not apologising for any of that.' His tone was rough, the gleam in his eyes dark and dangerous. 'I'm not apologising for dragging you off the stage because your behaviour at the engagement party was shocking. And if I've been mean it's because you seem to have no concept of boundaries. You swim in my fountain and you make free use of my recording studio—'

'Whoa!' Izzy recoiled. 'So what *are* you apologising for?'

'For not recognising your talent sooner. I can't understand why I didn't notice it the night of the party.' He frowned thoughtfully. 'You were really pushing your voice, maybe it distorted the vocal.'

'Well, I was desperate for you to listen to me! But what you're basically saying is that you seriously underestimated me.'

His jaw tensed. 'Yes, I underestimated you.'

'*Seriously* underestimated me?'

'I try to resist the overuse of adverbs.'

She smiled sweetly, enjoying the moment. 'In other words you find it tough to admit you're wrong.'

He ignored that. 'Have you ever worked with a record producer? Used a recording studio?'

'Only when I did *Singing Star* and that was

a disaster as everyone is always reminding me. Usually I do it myself. I saved up for some software. It's got a midi sequencer and audio recording so sometimes I use that. I tried songwriting software but it kept generating melodies I thought were rubbish. Occasionally I go along to the local sixth form college—they have a basic recording studio I can use.' Izzy was just eyeing the bathroom and wondering if she could surreptitiously disappear and put on some make-up when the prince took her hand and pulled her towards the door.

'We have work to do.'

'Now? It's three in the morning, and—' *I'm dressed in my pyjamas*, she thought, but the prince was already propelling her out of the door, displaying a level of energy lesser mortals could only envy. 'Where are we going?' She lowered her voice as she jogged alongside him. 'I hope we don't bump into anyone. This is *too* embarrassing.'

'Everyone is asleep. And we're going to my office. I want to play some tracks to you.' He flicked on a light, strode over to his desk and hit a button on the computer. Music throbbed through the office. 'I want your opinion.' He sprawled in the chair and her eyes slid to his long, powerful legs.

This was the first time she'd seen him casually dressed but the soft shirt and black jeans simply added to his sex appeal.

Izzy struggled to keep her mind on the task in hand. 'No one has ever asked my opinion on anything before.'

'I'm asking for it now.'

She listened and pulled a face. 'Truthfully? It's awful.'

'Why?'

'Because it's so depressing it makes me want to slit my own throat. I assume that's not the effect you're looking for.'

The tightening of his mouth suggested that it wasn't. 'I'm looking for emotional.'

'Miserable and emotional are *not* the same thing.' Suddenly worried that her pyjamas might be see-though under the lights, she sprang onto the soft couch in the corner of his office and tucked her legs under her. 'If I'm supposed to give an opinion, you'd better start by telling me what this song is *for*?'

'It's the charity single to be released ahead of this year's Rock 'n' Royal concert.'

Her stomach flipped as she realised he was involving her in something of enormous importance. 'So you need something with instant appeal that people are going to want to download straightaway. Unless they're contemplating suicide, it isn't going to be that track you just played. Is that all you've got?' She tried to focus on the music and not the shadow darkening his jaw or those long strong fingers resting on his thigh. She should have felt exhausted but instead she felt more alive than she could ever remember feeling.

He played another track and she instantly shook her head. 'The phrasing is wrong. The whole thing is too…too…*waffly.* I think they've tried to keep it interesting by avoiding repetition but they've managed to produce something that just isn't memorable. You want something that people are going to be singing in the bath and in their car. What you have is instantly forgettable. Next.' She could have sat there all night with him, listening to music and exchanging opinions with that warm glow inside her and the almost euphoric feeling of happiness.

He played another track and a hard, pounding rhythm filled the room.

Izzy winced. 'It's a good track to have sex to,

but I'm presuming that isn't the effect you're going for.' She spoke without thinking and their eyes met.

Shaken by the raw power of the attraction, Izzy pressed herself back against the sofa and wished she'd dressed in something more sophisticated than frog pyjamas.

Again he switched the track but Izzy was finding it harder and harder to concentrate on anything except the man sprawled on the other side of the room.

'So?' He switched off the final track and the sudden silence intensified the electric atmosphere of the room.

'None of those is right.'

'I agree.' He was silent for a moment, his eyes narrowed as he watched her. 'I know what I want.'

So did she.

She forgot all about the music and the fact that this was her dream. She forgot about the Rock 'n' Royal concert. She forgot about everything except the man. 'Yes.'

'I want your song.'

Her mind in a completely different place, Izzy gaped at him. 'My *song*?'

'Yes.'

'You want me to sing my song as this year's charity single?'

'No. I want to give it to someone else to sing.'

Aware that she'd been microseconds away from making a gigantic fool of herself, Izzy found her hands were shaking. 'Wow. I think that's the equivalent of patting someone on the head and punching them at the same time. I don't know whether I'm supposed to be ecstatic or outraged.' Or bitterly disappointed that he didn't want her, he wanted her song.

'*You* should be singing it. I'm not denying that, but it isn't just about the song, it's about the artist. I need a name.' His words were as blunt as his delivery. 'This is going to be big. An unknown artist singing an unknown song just won't cut it. You know that.'

'So you're basically saying, "We love your song, Izzy, but we think you suck so you can't sing it."'

'You do not suck. But nor do you have the profile we need to give this track instant appeal. Since you clearly have a great deal more commercial brainpower than everyone around you appreciates, I'm sure you understand that.'

'Yes.' She looked at him, torn. 'Yes, I understand that. But it's *my* song. I wrote it for me.' It was *about* her. It had significance. It was personal.

Look at me, I'm not what you see.

'Do you want your song heard by half the world, sung by a famous artist or do you want to keep it yourself to sing in the bath?'

'Ow, that's brutal.'

'You said you appreciate honesty.'

'I thought I did but maybe I was wrong about that.' Even knowing that he was speaking sense, she hung on to her song as if it were part of her. Surely if there was one thing worse than singing someone else's crappy song, it would be hearing someone else putting their own interpretation on a song she'd written for herself?

Or maybe not.

Her career was pretty much dead. She needed to do *something*.

Maybe it didn't matter that she wasn't the one singing it as long as the whole world was downloading it. The truth was she was finding it harder and harder to think about the song because all she could think about was *him*.

Misinterpreting her silence, he launched into an argument to convince her. 'Music executives get sent thousands of tracks daily. Tracks they don't even listen to. For someone with no contacts the chances of breaking into the business are one in a million. It's all word of mouth—who you know. If an A&R person says "listen to this" then they listen. A songwriter can't just write songs, they have to know how to market themselves—to get their music heard. This is your chance.'

'People aren't interested in who writes the songs.'

'They're going to be interested in this one because it's going to be everywhere.'

He was so confident. Not arrogant, she realised. Just self-assured.

Cautiously, she tested the flavour of his idea. 'Who do you have in mind to sing it?'

'Callie. She's moving towards a more contemporary sound and it would be perfect for her.'

Izzy had to agree. 'I love her voice. I have all her albums.'

'But?'

'I can't imagine she needs a song from me. She might say no.'

'She won't. She's looking for something a bit different and her own creative well has dried up. She's going to love this.' His phone was already in his hand and he raised his eyebrows. 'Is it a yes? Because there's a lot to do. I need to get a team on to it—not just the recording people but the lawyers…everyone. This is huge, Izzy, but we have to move fast.'

Izzy's head was buzzing.

Her song.

The song she'd written with nothing but her imagination and her voice.

Matteo rose to his feet. 'You're exhausted. Get some sleep. We'll talk about it tomorrow.' He walked towards the door and opened it.

Izzy watched him for a moment and then slid off the couch and walked towards him, summoning as much dignity as a woman could when wearing frog pyjamas. 'She can sing my song.'

'Good decision.' His arm brushed against hers and that brief touch was all it took. Liquid longing poured through her, heating her body from head to foot.

Having spent the past hour watching him she was so revved up her body was on fire. She desperately wanted him to kiss her again but at the same time she didn't.

Her last relationship had been an absolute disaster.

The fallout had affected her for months.

He stepped back from her quickly and Izzy caught his eye.

'OK, this is crazy. Do you have any idea why we feel like this? Because honestly, if you know please tell me so I can talk myself out of it.'

Until she'd met him she'd never known that sexual attraction could be this powerful.

With a soft curse he slid his fingers under her chin and lifted her face to his. For a moment he looked down at her and all she could think about were his fingers, warm and strong against her face, and the fact that her heart was sprinting inside her chest.

She could hardly breathe. 'I don't know why I feel like this because honestly you drive me nuts.'

'You drive me nuts too.' His eyes darkened and she saw her own conflict reflected in his gaze.

His head lowered slightly, or maybe it was just her imagination because she wanted it so badly. The memory of the way he kissed turned her thoughts to a foggy pulp and sent a dragging ache through the base of her belly. Breathless anticipation became a wicked hunger and her willpower, her self-control and her 'goals' all retreated to a place where they were no longer accessible.

'*Cristo*, you're right. We can't do this.' His voice

hoarse, he took a step backwards, wincing as he crashed into the wall behind. 'You'd better go. Go now.'

Her head still spinning, Izzy stared at him dizzily. 'Yes.' She tried to walk but her legs wouldn't move. 'Just for the record, this is because I'm a tacky popstar and you're a prince, right?'

'No.' His jaw was clenched and his eyes were two narrow slits. 'This is because you're young and you have a romantic view of relationships.'

'There's something wrong with believing in romance?'

'Not at all,' he drawled, 'providing those views are shared by the man in question. You believe in love and happy ever afters. Your view of the world is based on a fairy tale. I, on the other hand, am a grim realist. I'm jaded and cynical. Any relationship between us would be guaranteed to end in heartbreak.'

'Given that you're reputed not to have a heart, I presume it's my heart that's going to be breaking in this scenario.'

'Yes. And my ideal woman doesn't have a heart to break.'

'Apart from the fact that one of my goals is to avoid emotional involvement, you're *so* not my type there just isn't any way I'd fall in love with you.'

A sardonic smile touched his mouth. 'A risk I'm not prepared to take.'

'You think you're that irresistible? That really is arrogant.'

'For once I was being unselfish, but if you wish to call it arrogance that doesn't worry me. You've already been hurt once. I'm not about to do it a second time.'

Humiliation washed over her and her face caught fire. 'You know about that?'

'I saw the pictures of you crying on the steps of the church.'

'Oh, great.'

His mouth twitched. 'The dress was hideous.'

The comment made her laugh. 'Yes, it was. Rhinestones. God, what was I thinking? It was worse than red sequins. Maybe that's why he didn't turn up.' Swallowing back the hurt, she gave a weak smile. 'No, actually he didn't turn up because my record bombed and I was no longer a useful person to be associated with. He used me. And I suppose I shouldn't mind about that given my own track record, except that at least I'm honest about it. Who would have thought we would have so much in common? Anyway, that's enough of my sob story. What's yours?'

'Why do you assume I have a sob story?'

'A prince who doesn't believe in happy endings? Something must have gone wrong in your fairy tale.' The temptation to reach out and touch him was almost overwhelming. She was fascinated by the brief glimpse of bronzed skin at the neck of his shirt. 'So what happened, Your Highness? You loved her too much? Not enough? She broke your heart? You broke hers?'

The change in him was instantaneous.

It was as if he'd slammed the door in her face.

'You need to go to bed.' His voice was raw and her heart turned over with a yearning for the impossible.

'So you prefer meaningless relationships.'

'That's what I do, and I do it well.'

She was absolutely sure he'd do it supremely well and just the thought of it made her knees weak. His fingers were still touching her cheek and she willed him to slide his hand behind her head and bring his mouth down on hers.

'What if I told you I prefer meaningless relationships too?'

'I'd know you were lying.' There was a long silence and then he breathed deeply and stepped back from her. '*Buonanotte*, Izzy. Go to bed and dream of happy endings because that's all they are. Dreams. In the morning we'll see what we can do about that other dream of yours.'

CHAPTER SIX

IN THE end she dreamed of princes. Or rather, of one prince in particular. But her dreams didn't involve marriage. Instead she was singing live at the Rock 'n' Royal concert in front of millions of people and the prince was trying to drag her off the stage. Her red sequined dress split under the strain and she was left standing naked in front of half the world.

Relieved to wake up, Izzy dragged herself to the bathroom to splash her face and clear her head.

Any relationship between us would be bound to end in heartbreak.

He was right.

She'd known him for less than three days and she'd woken up thinking of him rather than her daily goal. That had to be a bad thing.

As she pulled on a turquoise skirt and strappy top she'd bought specially for the holiday, she tried to focus on the fact that one of the hottest artists in the US was going to sing her song.

This was her dream, wasn't it?

Well, half her dream. It was her song, even if she wasn't the one singing it.

She should have been dancing with excitement, instead of which she just kept thinking about how his mouth had felt on hers.

She was sitting on the edge of the bed when there was a tap on the door and one of the prince's household staff entered.

'His Royal Highness has asked for you to go straight to the helipad, *signorina*. The helicopter is waiting.'

'Helicopter?' Izzy's stomach flipped. He was sending her home. He'd decided it wasn't a good idea having her here and he didn't even have the guts to tell her himself.

Under the sick disappointment, anger fizzed. He had his song and now he wanted her out of the way. Determined to keep her dignity, she stood. 'It's going to take me five minutes to pack my things. I'll be down in a minute.'

The man gave her an apologetic look. 'His Highness was most insistent that you leave immediately, *signorina*.'

So he wanted her out of here so fast he wasn't even going to let her pack.

Feeling really fed up and angry, she followed the man to the helipad and boarded the helicopter, furious with herself for feeling the hot sting of tears.

'*Buongiorno,*' the prince's deep, sexy voice greeted her from the helicopter, and Izzy was thrown because she hadn't expected him to be there in person and she'd spent the past few minutes building him up into a monster in her head.

He handed her a helmet. 'Put this on.'

The fury in her died as she met his eyes. *She didn't want to leave.* 'It'll ruin my hair,' she muttered, 'do I have to?'

'While I'm the one at the controls, yes.'

'You're flying it?' She jammed the helmet on her head. 'Why are you flying me yourself? Are you afraid I'll ask them to land somewhere else? Do a runner on the way home?'

'You're not going home. And I always fly myself.'

'I'm not going home?'

'Of course not. Why would you think that?' Reaching out, he adjusted her helmet. 'Is that comfortable?'

'No, but never mind.' She didn't even care. As long as she wasn't going home, she didn't care about anything. Feeling lighter inside, Izzy settled herself in the helicopter. 'At least you're not giving me a lift in a fast jet. I should be grateful for small mercies. Am I going to be sick?'

'You drank all that champagne and managed not to be sick so I have high hopes for you,' he drawled. 'Get in. We're already late.'

'I don't even know where we're going.' Izzy looked at the instruments. 'I hope you know what you're doing because I'm too young to die in a crumpled heap of mangled metal.'

With an exasperated shake of his head, he fastened her harness and then his hands were on the controls, sure and steady, and she could hear his voice through the sound system in her helmet. 'We're going to visit the Roman amphitheatre at St Pietro d'Angelo. I'm meeting a few members of the committee to discuss final arrangements for the concert along with some of the production, light and sound crew. You've been nagging me to let you get involved with the concert—I thought you'd find it interesting.'

Izzy gripped her seat. 'I'm sure I will. If I live that long.'

'I thought you were gutsy.'

'I'm not good with fairground rides and I have a feeling this is going to be the same.'

'You're going to love it.' He shot her a brief look of amusement before concentrating on the controls.

Her stomach swooped as they rose into the air and she felt a lurch of fear that swiftly turned to wonder as the world shrank beneath them. 'Oh, it's fantastic! Like being a bird.' And her grin widened as he flew them across the island. 'I really, really thought you were sending me home.'

His eyes were fixed on the horizon. 'You're not going home, Izzy.'

Not yet.

Eventually she would, of course, but she wasn't going to think about that now. She wasn't going to let anything spoil this moment.

There was a wicked thrill involved in watching him—something inherently sexy about the way he handled the powerful machine. Maybe he *was* a touch arrogant and he certainly had a habit of commanding everyone around him, but having met so many useless, dependent men in her life she found his take-charge attitude a refreshing change. Power was an aphrodisiac, she realised, and suddenly she felt ridiculously happy.

'So how far is this amphitheatre?' Please let it be a long way so that she could stay in the air forever, with this incredible bird's-eye view. Beneath them lay silver sand beaches and dramatic cliffs, tiny fishing villages with houses in shades of pale rose and terracotta overlooking a translucent turquoise sea. As he flew inland the vista changed and she saw the remains of a ruined temple half hidden on the lush hillside. 'It's very green for a Mediterranean island.'

'Olive growing is a major industry here. If you look to your left now you have a perfect view of the amphitheatre.'

And there beneath her on top of the hill, resplendent in the sunlight, lay a thousand years of history and Izzy caught her breath because nothing had prepared her for something so spectacular.

Matteo's hands were steady on the controls as he landed. 'It was built by the Romans, at around the same time they built the amphitheatre in Verona. The acoustics are perfect. It's used for an opera festival in the summer and once a year we use it for the Rock 'n' Royal concert and the place is transformed. You won't recognise it. Tomorrow night there's a light and sound spectacular so the sound and lighting crew are treating it as a run-through for the concert.'

Izzy sat for a moment, wishing they could just take off again and keep flying.

'That was the best thing I've ever done. And it's the perfect thing to do for a control freak like you because you can fly yourself.'

'You're calling me a control freak?' He helped her release her harness. 'This from someone who has a Goal for the Day? Talking of which, what is your goal of today? Better let me know so that I can be prepared.'

'To resist you.'

Astonishment flared in his eyes. 'That's your goal?'

'Yes.' Her voice was a squeak. 'Since I met you I haven't managed to make a decent work-related goal. Apparently the chemistry messes with my brain, so first I have to resist you and then I can get my life back on track.' Izzy turned her head and stared at the amphitheatre. 'So they built a massive arena in the middle of nowhere. Why would they do a thing like that? How did every-one get here?'

'Izzy—'

'No, truly, I just want to talk about something

else.' She brushed her hair away from her face, wilting in the heat. 'And if you could be boring that would be extra helpful.'

'I'll do my best.' His low drawl played havoc with her nerve endings and as they walked up a narrow path towards the amphitheatre she gave herself a stern talking to.

She could not afford to be distracted by a man who had what it took to break her heart. It had been bad enough after Brian and he'd been a complete wimp.

'So to answer your question, the amphitheatre wasn't always in the middle of nowhere.' His eyes were concealed by a pair of sunglasses, but with or without dark glasses he was a man who commanded attention. 'There was originally a city here, but nothing remains now. It was built by an occupying Roman force to house their gladiatorial games.' He continued to tell her about the history and she tried hard to be bored but instead she was fascinated. And so were the people around them when it gradually dawned on the throngs of tourists that they had royalty in their midst.

Apparently oblivious to the buzzing excitement created by his presence, he strode towards a group of men waiting by the main entrance to the amphitheatre. Watching the exchange, Izzy realised that his role in the project was far more than just that of a figurehead.

He talked briefly to someone he introduced as the technical director and then to the systems technician before guiding Izzy through a stone archway.

The sheer scope of the ancient building was breathtaking, the seating rising upwards from an oval arena that shimmered under the hot sunshine. It was all too easy to imagine the sweat and fear of the gladiators as they prepared to fight to the death in front of an enormous crowd.

Izzy shivered. 'So they're going to rehearse here tonight?'

'Not a full technical rehearsal. They just want to try out some ideas. It is closed to the public from 6:00 p.m. this evening. The set construction and lighting rehearsals have taken place at an aircraft hangar at Santina Airport. Tonight they just want to play with some new ideas. The production manager and the lighting designer will be here soon.'

'I'd never given any thought to how much planning goes into a rock concert.'

'Lighting for this sort of live event is completely different from arenas or festivals.' He kept the conversation formal but that didn't alter the chemistry that pressed down on them like an invisible force. She noticed that he was keeping his distance. Not a casual distance that happened without thought, but a carefully contrived space, a deliberate barrier that emphasised the effort required to push back at what pulled them together.

'And all the money goes to your charity?' Izzy frowned. 'So if you do all the charity stuff, what does Alex do? I mean, I know he's the Crown Prince, but what does that mean?'

There was a long silence and Matteo stared across the arena. 'It means that eventually he gets landed with it all. The throne and the responsibility.'

Izzy let out a long breath. 'That's pretty heavy. No wonder he's enjoying his freedom. But presumably your parents think it's time he came home and got on with doing prince stuff.'

His mouth flickered. '"Prince stuff" covers a broad range of activities.'

'I'm starting to understand why the king and queen were welcoming to Allegra,' Izzy murmured. 'They think that if Alex is married, he'll settle down and come home.'

'They also think a royal wedding would be well received by the public.'

'But the public love you because you spend your time raising tons of money for worthy causes.' Having spent her life around selfish people and knowing that she was pretty self-centred herself, Izzy was humbled. 'You do a lot for other people. I don't do anything like that.'

'I don't have to earn a living. It's different.' He lifted his hand and brushed her hair away from her face.

Excitement shot through her and she wondered how such a simple gesture could have that effect on her. Her heart was banging against her chest and suddenly all she wanted was for him to kiss her again. 'So now you try and persuade rich, influential people to donate to your charity. The articles I read said something about your skills at international diplomacy, which is basically saying the right thing at the right time, isn't it? I don't think I'd be very good at that.'

'You're probably right.' His smile was faintly mocking. 'You, Izzy Jackson, are a walking diplomatic incident.'

Remembering her behaviour the night of the party, she coloured. 'I'm sorry I drank too much.

I'm sorry I sang. I'm sorry I argued with you and forgot to turn off the microphone.'

'I'm not.' He was the embodiment of masculine virility, standing there with his jet-black hair gleaming under the Mediterranean sun. Suddenly she couldn't breathe and her mind raced to all sorts of places it shouldn't have been going.

'Y-you're not?'

'If that hadn't happened I wouldn't have heard your voice or that song.'

She might have believed that was the only reason had it not been for the edge to his tone and the tension visible in his broad shoulders.

Deciding that they both needed distraction, Izzy shielded her eyes from the sun and stared at the top seats. 'Are we allowed to climb up there?'

'It's hot. Do you want to?'

'Yes. Although I might pass out. The only exercise I get is dancing and I haven't been doing a lot of that lately.' But anything had to be better than standing here waiting to be incinerated by the explosive blast of sexual chemistry.

Trying to outrun it she sprinted up the first few steps and was soon gasping for air.

Fixing her gaze on the top, Izzy ploughed on. 'Must have been hell being a spectator here in

Roman times,' she panted, 'but at least if I crash to the bottom I won't be eaten by lions.'

Not even out of breath, he glanced at her in amusement. 'I've never met anyone as determined as you.'

'It's one of my biggest faults. As a toddler I was determined to climb out of my cot and I didn't give up until I managed it—and broke my arm.' She flopped down onto the top step and tried to suck air into her screaming lungs. 'I need to start using the gym or something. I'm full of good intentions but something always gets in the way.'

'You think being determined is a fault?' He sat down next to her, his leg brushing against hers. 'I see it as a quality. Life is hard. Without determination it's almost impossible to achieve anything. You have tremendous drive and focus.'

Izzy realised that despite all the empty space, they'd ended up sitting close together. He was staring down into the arena where the team was working but she sensed that he was no more engaged with what was going on than she was and the raw chemistry terrified her because she'd never felt anything like it before.

He looked at her at the same time she looked at

him and that single wordless exchange intensified the feverish burning inside her.

Izzy's limbs trembled. However powerful the attraction, this was a man who didn't give anything of himself emotionally and she'd be foolish to forget that.

'Tell me about your relationship with this Katarina woman.' The words blurted out of her before she could stop them.

'How do you know about Katarina?' His tone lowered the temperature between them by several degrees and she made a mental note that if she wanted to defuse the heat all she had to do was throw in a personal question.

'I read something…' She kept her answer purposefully vague and his jaw tightened.

'You should know better than to believe what you read.'

The fact that she was desperate to ask if it was serious really unsettled her because she knew it shouldn't matter. 'Look—they're waving at you. You'd better go down and see what they want. I'll stay here.'

The next few hours passed in a whirl of technical preparations, most of which Izzy just observed from a distance. She imagined how it must feel to sing here in front of a crowd of tens of thousands of people. She imagined the darkness, the lights and the excitement of having that many people listening to her.

One day, she promised herself. One day she'd write something so brilliant that it was impossible for people not to take her seriously. And then she felt horribly shallow thinking only of herself and her own career when Matteo's whole life appeared to have been dedicated to duty and responsibility.

She had no idea how long she sat there lost in her thoughts, but suddenly she was aware that he was back by her side and that the light had faded.

The tourists had long since left the arena and only the lighting technicians remained, preparing for the light and sound show that would take place the following night.

His knee brushed against hers and she gave a little shiver because even that minimal contact was enough to destabilise her.

'Cold?' His voice was rough and Izzy shook her head.

'No.' This time she kept her eyes forward. 'Just imagining how it will be with a crowd of fifty thousand.'

He didn't answer immediately and she knew

he wasn't thinking of the crowd any more than she was.

The urge to touch him was so powerful it was almost painful.

Hidden in the shadows of darkness while the lights played beneath them, Izzy couldn't help herself. She reached out a hand towards him and was just a millionth of a second away from touching him when common sense gave her the red light. She was about to pull back when her hand was captured by warm, male fingers. And his touch felt so spectacularly good that she couldn't pull away.

Crazy, she thought. Crazy to feel this way when the man was just holding her hand.

He pressed her hand to his thigh and her palm was trapped against hard male muscle. She felt warmth and power and excitement, and awareness slammed into her.

Suddenly she was holding her breath, wanting desperately for him to kiss her again.

And then his fingers captured her chin and he turned her face to his. For a brief moment she saw the blaze of raw passion in his eyes and then his head lowered to hers. The anticipation was so sharp it was almost painful. His lips touched hers gently, teased and tasted, and she gave a low moan because this had been what she'd wanted since that first night in the turret bedroom.

Her arms slid round his neck just as a beam of light tracked towards them, dazzling them both.

His head jerked back and he was on his feet. *'Cristo!'*

Izzy was dazed. How had they—? 'That was *your* fault,' she croaked, and he jabbed his fingers through his hair.

'Maybe, but—'

'Look, I don't want it to happen any more than you do.' As jumpy as a kangaroo, she shot out of her seat. 'I have plans. Goals. Hot sex with you is nowhere on my list.'

In the semi-darkness, his eyes met hers and that look brushed every part of her until her skin was hot and her breathing shallow.

Izzy gulped. 'I'm getting vertigo up here, so I'm going down.'

His hand closed over hers, his fingers warm and strong. 'If you're dizzy someone should hold on to you.'

'Unless that someone is the reason for the dizziness.' Her heartbeat going crazy, Izzy extracted her hand from his in the hope that it might help. 'If it's OK with you I've had enough of this romantic darkness. I'm going to go and stand in a spotlight. You should do the same thing. It might help me to focus on your deficiencies.' Without waiting for his response, she picked her way down the steps as fast as she dared in the fragmented light.

It would have been so easy to lose her footing and plunge down, down, and part of her felt as if she was about to do exactly that. Ironically she managed the steps perfectly well but then lost her balance on the uneven floor of the arena.

Strong hands caught her as she stumbled and the next moment he'd swept her into the shadow of a stone pillar, away from the intrusive sweep of the lights.

Instead of releasing her, his hands tightened on her shoulders.

'I have never wanted a woman the way I want you.' His raw confession acted like a shot of adrenalin and suddenly her heart was pounding.

'I feel the same way.'

'I don't *like* feeling this desperate!' The words were dragged from him but even as he spoke, his hand locked in her hair and he powered her back against the nearest hard surface which just happened to be the pillar.

Trapped between rough stone and his hard body, Izzy barely had time to suck in a shocked breath before his mouth came down on hers and he was kissing her with such unrestrained sexual hunger that her body erupted in a burst of flame. This time there was no tantalizing exploration but a full on assault of her senses, the erotic stroke of his tongue deliberate and explicit as his mouth possessed hers and showered sensation over every millimetre of her trembling body.

She'd always prided herself on being in control of her responses but she'd never been kissed like this before and his expertise smashed down every feeble barrier until she was a seething mass of shivering, quivering desire.

Somehow his hands had moved from her hair to her bottom, trapping her against the hard heat of his arousal, and her arms were around his neck as they both instinctively tried to connect every single part of themselves. The sun had set hours earlier so the air had cooled, but their bodies were slick with sweat as they drove each other wild. Desire was thick and molten, dark and dangerous, unheeding of time or place.

His breathing was laboured, and as his hands slid beneath the thin fabric of her top she gave a whimper of encouragement and then jerked as his thumbs boldly traced the straining peaks of her breasts. On fire, Izzy moaned against the heat of his mouth but he was already ahead of her, dispensing with her bra with expert fingers and then employing those same skilled fingers on her sensitive peaks until the ache between her thighs grew almost unbearable.

A beam of light tracked towards them again and with a rough curse he shifted her further into the shadows, using the pillar to protect them from the intrusive beam of the spotlight.

Izzy moaned. 'Someone might see—'

'I don't care if the whole damn Roman army is watching.' His thickened tone was barely intelligible and then he was kissing her again, his mouth hard on hers, hot and hungry, the lick of his tongue a blatant prelude to an intimacy she craved as much as he clearly did.

She covered him with the flat of her hand and heard him groan.

He slid his hand under her skirt, his fingers finding their target with unerring accuracy.

Sure, clever fingers traced that secret part of her and the pleasure was so crazily intense that she would have cried out had he not already had his mouth on hers.

Drowning in an overload of sensation, she forgot everything except *this*. Here, behind the cloaking shadow of the ancient pillar it was just the two of them and the contrast between their private world, and the swirling lights of the auditorium somehow added to the intimacy. And it *was* intimate. What had started as a kiss swiftly exploded into something deeply primitive as the fire between them burned through the restraints they'd imposed on themselves.

Izzy was so lost in that kiss, so focused on what he was doing with his mouth and his fingers, that it came as a shock to feel his hands slide under the flimsy barrier of her skirt and close hard over her trembling thighs.

They were both out of control. Both past the point of caring about consequences.

She was so desperate that even as a tiny sane part of her brain was reminding herself that they couldn't possibly do *that* in such a public place, she felt his fingers rip the elastic of her panties.

Crazy excitement collided with shock.

Surely he wasn't actually going to—

Oh, goodness, he was....

Dark, intense and terrifying, it consumed them and drove them as they raced towards the inevitable like addicts with no thought to the past or the future. Izzy was a seething mass of sensation. Her pelvis ached, the explosive heat engulfing her as he explored her with erotic precision and careless disregard for their surroundings.

Quivering from head to toe, Izzy's thoughts blurred. Part of her wanted to stop him, to point out that perhaps they should go somewhere more private, but another part of her was desperate for him *not* to stop and she wasn't at all sure she would have been able to anyway. And yes, there was the extra thrill that came from being wanted this badly, by this man.

She felt him lift her and she locked her legs behind his back.

She felt his arousal—smooth, silken hardness against the soft flesh of her inner thigh.

The beam of light tracked towards them again, and again he shifted skilfully, avoiding its path without allowing the threat of exposure to distract him from his purpose.

He supported her easily, the muscles of his powerful shoulders bunched and, as he took her weight, his intention explicit in the deliberate shift of his hands.

Shock sliced through excitement as she realised he was going to take her right there—fast and hard, sex at its most basic, an expression of the most primitive human need—even as she acknowledged that her body was already going along with that, caught up in the same wild craving that was consuming him.

But even as everything in her caught fire, a small part of her brain came back to life, ignited by some sense of self-preservation too powerfully ingrained to be completely silenced even in circumstances as intense as these.

Poised on the edge of oblivion, Izzy tried to speak but his mouth was on hers and the heat of that kiss shimmered through her, muting sound.

She flattened her hands on his shoulders and tried again.

No sound emerged but something must have communicated itself to him because for a fraction of a second he paused and that brief interlude was enough to shake her out of the sexual trance that gripped her.

'No.' Her voice was barely audible. 'No—'

His eyes were black as night. 'Izzy—'

'Condom.' It was all she could manage to say and she could have sobbed with frustration when he froze because, although they had to stop, she didn't want to. She desperately hoped he'd just reach into his pocket and whip out the goods but he stayed utterly still, as if unable to move, his breathing harsh and uneven.

Then he lowered her gently to the ground and pushed her skirt down. For a moment he stayed still, his forehead resting against his arm as he struggled for control. Then he breathed deeply and hauled himself away from her, turning so that she couldn't see his face.

She had no idea what he was thinking but she had a fair idea.

'Matteo—'

'Just…give me a minute.'

Her body was shimmering with unfulfilled sexual need and her treacherous libido was urging her to grab him and drag him back to her but he turned suddenly, his mouth a grim line in the shadowed darkness. Apart from one missing button on his shirt there was no outward evidence of their close encounter.

'We need to leave.'

'But—'

'Now.'

'All right.' Except that it wasn't all right and she didn't want to go back. Part of her wished she hadn't said anything, but even as that thought flew into her head, she dismissed it. Decisions had consequences and an unplanned pregnancy wasn't romantic; it was foolish and irresponsible. Her face scarlet, she retrieved her torn panties and stuffed them in her pocket.

Life wasn't black and white, Izzy thought numbly as she picked her way through the darkness. Hers was a massive lump of grey.

They boarded the helicopter in silence.

Not one word was spoken throughout the flight. When they landed, he sprang from the helicopter, waiting just long enough to check that she was safely on the ground and clear of the deadly blades before striding in the direction of his office with no more than a curt goodnight.

Anger replacing passion, Izzy paused only briefly and then stalked after him.

If he thought they were just going to pretend it hadn't happened then he had another think coming.

Inside his offices he flipped on a light and

then opened a cupboard and pulled out a bottle of whisky.

Izzy stood in the door, anger mingling with vulnerability. She didn't regret stopping him but she did regret the sudden shift in their relationship. Their fledgling friendship had been crushed under the weight of more powerful emotions.

'I've driven you to drink already? That was quick, even for me. Usually it takes more than a couple of days.' Flippancy didn't hide her misery and she bit her lip. 'Look, I'm sorry, but—'

'Why are you sorry? You did the right thing. The sensible thing.' His voice raw, he sloshed liquid into a glass and drank. 'I'm not in the habit of indulging in public sex. I assume you're not either.'

Izzy forced herself to breathe slowly. This was nowhere near as bad as discovering that your fiancé had only proposed to get his picture in all the tabloids, so why did she feel as if someone had removed her insides with a sharp implement? Feeling sick, she watched as he topped up his glass. 'You're going to have the mother of all hangovers tomorrow.'

'That's my business.'

'That's it?' Her voice rose. 'That's all you're going to say?'

'There's nothing more to say. I lost control. That's it.'

Regret mingled with misery, forming a dark, swirling mass of horrible feelings in her stomach. What had she expected? That he'd sort out the whole protection issue and carry on where they'd left off?

The moment had gone.

They no longer had the seductive darkness of the amphitheatre as an excuse for sexual madness. The lights were on and they were both sober. 'Right. I'll just leave you to beat yourself up about losing control then.'

The fact that he didn't have a single gentle word to soften the hardness hurt her deeply, but still, if he'd made a move towards her she would have willingly gone to him because she was as shaken by the encounter as he was, but he made no move.

Even when she walked towards the door, nothing.

Turning the handle, Izzy paused for a fraction of a second. But still he made no move, so she walked from the room without looking back.

CHAPTER SEVEN

MEN!

There was nothing quite like a man to mess with your head and throw everything off course. Furious with herself, Izzy stuffed her clothes into her suitcase. She was going home. And she was going to create a man-free exclusion zone and focus on her work.

Eyes gritty after yet another sleepless night, she zipped the case and dragged it bumping behind her down the curving, ornate staircase.

It seemed impossible to believe she'd only been at the palazzo for a few days. It felt as if her whole life had changed. And yet how could she possibly stay now? It would just be hideously embarrassing for both of them. Ignoring the heavy ache inside her, she focused on practicalities—booking a flight, getting to the airport, dodging the press. She thought about where she was going to go when she arrived back in England. The only thing she was careful not to think about was what had almost happened the night before.

Maybe one day, when it wasn't likely to hurt any more, she'd retrieve the thought from her brain, polish it up and enjoy the memory. Right now she didn't dare look at it.

Abandoning her case in the middle of the floor, she stalked off in search of Matteo.

Serena informed her that he was working out in the gym and that it wasn't wise to disturb him, but Izzy reasoned that their relationship couldn't exactly deteriorate any further and there was no way she was running away like a coward without facing him.

Plenty of women would have slunk away but she'd never been one to slink anywhere.

She strode over to the gym complex expecting to find him on a row of treadmills pounding away. Instead she saw a boxing ring and the prince stripped to the waist, muscles pumped up and hard and gleaming with sweat as he fought another man of similar build.

Izzy was so shocked that for a moment she couldn't move.

Without the concealing properties of precision tailoring, there was no hiding the raw masculinity and primitive sex appeal. Nor was it any longer possible to block out the memories of the night before.

Leaning against the wall for support, she stared as the man she'd thought of as cold and restrained threw hard, lethal punches at his opponent. Even she, ignorant about boxing, could see that the prince was stronger and his skill superior. His torso was hard and muscled, not overbuilt like a bodybuilder, but super-fit and strong as he put himself through a demanding training routine. He was light on his feet and lethally accurate, and there was no missing the explosive power behind each punch he threw.

She'd known he was strong, of course. There were the times he'd scooped her up and carried her, and then there was last night when he'd supported her weight easily when they'd almost made love.

Not 'made love,' Izzy corrected herself instantly. They'd almost had sex. She was determined not to spin warm fantasies out of cold reality.

His bronzed shoulders gleamed with the sweat of hard physical exertion and Izzy couldn't shake the feeling that he was punishing himself rather than his opponent. Like a relentless machine, he threw punch after punch. Either he had extraordinary reserves of energy or he hadn't been lying awake all night as she had.

She had no idea how long she stood there watching but while she did something inside her shifted and reshaped because she realised that there were different sides to this man. She'd caught glimpses of it the night he'd dragged her off the stage and again the night before when he'd flattened her to the cold stone of the ancient pillar.

Superior strength and skill gave him the upper hand and Izzy winced as he knocked the other man to the ground. Or maybe she actually made a sound because he lifted his head, those stormy eyes narrowing as he noticed her for the first time.

'Izzy?'

He vaulted the ropes and she took an involuntary step backwards. After what had happened the night before she didn't trust herself to be that close to him, especially when he was looking like a modern-day version of Hercules.

'How long have you been standing there? I gave orders I wasn't to be disturbed.' He reached for a towel he'd slung over a bench and draped it round his neck. His muscles were pumped up and hard and her mouth dried because she'd had her hands on those muscles and she wanted to put her hands on them again. And because she was desperate to stroke and touch, she kept her eyes fixed on his face and didn't look at his body.

'I wanted to see you before I left.'

'Left?' Frowning, he reached for a bottle of water. 'Where are you going?'

'Home.' It was hard to concentrate when all she really wanted to do was feast her eyes on gleaming bronzed skin and vibrant masculinity. 'This just isn't working out for either of us.'

The prince turned to his opponent, who had been hovering at a respectful distance, and said something in Italian that must have been a dismissal because the man melted away, leaving the two of them alone.

Izzy watched him go with mixed feelings. 'You knocked him down and you didn't even say sorry.'

'He knocked me down in yesterday's session.' Unapologetic, Matteo drank. 'It's training. It's not personal.'

'You did this yesterday?'

'I box every day.'

'Why?'

He lowered the bottle slowly. 'Fitness training. And, Izzy, you're not going home.'

'Most people just use treadmills and weights,' Izzy said absently. 'And I am going home. If you were a decent person you'd be considering my feelings and not just your own.'

'I *am* considering your feelings.'

Tense and exhausted, Izzy exploded. 'No, you're not! If you were considering my feelings you would have given me a big hug last night or said something nice and caring, instead of which you stood as far away from me as possible and proceeded to make me feel smaller than plankton.' She registered the astonishment in his eyes and ploughed on. '*Not* that I was expecting much, but something a bit complimentary would have been nice and presumably there must have been *something* you liked about me or you wouldn't have had almost-sex with me in the first place, and to go from that to realising that the man you've just had almost-sex with is only thinking about himself is frankly really depressing. It's not easy keeping your self-esteem intact in this world where so many people want to put you down. So basically I'm leaving before I develop performance anxiety and while I still have the confidence to travel unaccompanied.' Hating herself for being so open when he was so closed, Izzy went to stalk past him but he took a step and blocked her path.

'Last night I was *not* thinking about myself.'

'Yes, you were! You felt remorse because you let your precious control slip, not because you cared about me. You were furious with yourself for dropping those rigid standards you're so proud of. And actually, it's all very confusing. You're like two different people. I get the occasional glimpse of this wild side of you, and by the way I quite like that side, and then you lock it down. What's wrong with losing control once in a while?'

'I don't have a wild side.'

'Tell that to a woman you haven't flattened against a pillar.' Still not looking at him, she tried to push her way past him but he didn't budge. 'Excuse me!'

'I've really upset you.' His voice was deep and rough and played havoc with her insides.

'Yes, you have upset me. Now move before I hurt you.' *Before I give in and look.* 'And don't think those muscles will save you because there are moves I know.'

There was a pause and then she felt his hands close over her arms.

'You know moves?' His fingers were gentle and

there was a hint of humour in his tone. 'Are those the same moves you showed me last night?'

Her heart rate accelerated at an alarming rate. 'You had your chance to talk about last night and you blew it. Now we're just going to forget it.'

'I hope you're having more success at that than I am.' His fingers slid under her chin and he gently lifted her face. 'You're not leaving, Izzy.'

'You kept me here because you were worried the press would be more interested in me than my sister, but that's all fine now. The whole country is excited about the engagement. Everyone is happy and I'm going to go home and keep a low profile. And that's fine. Frankly I'm fed up with being a national joke....' Finally she looked at him and her voice trailed off as she noticed the vicious-looking scar that puckered the skin on his other-wise smooth, muscular torso. It started under his ribs and carried on around his back. *How could she not have noticed that before?* 'What...what happened to you?' Shocked, Izzy lifted a hand to touch the scar but he released her instantly and stepped back, his expression blank.

'Nothing.'

'You see? You're doing it again.' The fact that he didn't trust her hurt more than anything that had gone before. 'You know every sordid detail of my life and I haven't even bothered to try and hide it, but when I ask you about yours you lock it all down and tell me "nothing," but it must have been a hell of a nothing to leave scars like those.' She breathed deeply, wondering why her emotions were always so exaggerated around this man. 'I'm leaving because I'm not getting anything done here and because this whole thing is getting too complicated. Good luck with the concert.'

Just about maintaining her dignity, she shot past him out of the door but she'd barely gone five steps when he spoke.

'You want to know about the scars?' His tone was harsh. 'They happened the one and only time I trusted someone. I was eighteen years old and so arrogant I was blind to everything except my own importance. She was thirty. Sophisticated, intelligent—or so I thought. The attraction was instant. I was young, governed by testosterone and not much else. I was a prince and I had no idea what to do about that. My brother was the heir. I had no role apart from finding new ways to enjoy myself. I thought I could take whatever I wanted.'

Izzy swallowed. 'And you wanted her?'

'I chased after her like a stallion after a mare

and she refused to be caught. It was months before I could see what a clever game she'd played.'

Izzy winced because it was so easy to predict
what was coming. 'Social climber?'

The sun glinted off his dark hair. 'At first I
didn't think so. She refused to be seen with me
in public. She was almost ridiculously discreet. I
thought she was perfect. Turned out she was keeping her best till last.'

He was silent for so long she was about to
prompt him but then he spoke. 'I was about to
leave to take up my place at Cambridge University
when the package arrived.'

'What was in the package?'

'A film she'd made of us having sex. Revealing
photographs. And with it the blackmail. Pay or
else.'

It was all so horribly predictable. 'Kiss and sell.
What did you do?'

'The worst thing anyone can do in that situation. I tried to fix it myself. I was young and very
angry.' His voice was soft. 'I arranged to meet her
in a secluded place to talk about our relationship.
I wanted to make sense of it.'

Izzy's heart clenched. Hadn't she felt the same
way when useless Brian had dumped her? 'You

can't make sense of someone else's manipulative behaviour.'

'I was furious, humiliated, appalled that I'd put myself and my family in this position.' He ran his hand over his face and breathed out slowly. 'I arrived at the summer house where we'd been meeting in secret. I had one security officer with me because when we were growing up we were never allowed to go anywhere without a body-guard in tow. He was supposed to wait at a discreet distance.' There was a brief pause. 'I told her that she disgusted me and that I'd never pay her a penny. And that was when her brother appeared. My security officer. The man appointed by my father and assigned to protect me.'

Izzy stared. 'She was his sister?'

'They'd plotted it between them. They expected me to pay. I refused. Turned out that was another bad decision on my part, although I did give him more trouble than he'd anticipated.' The brevity of description together with the scars she'd seen on his torso told her just how severe that beating must have been.

'Who rescued you?'

'They left me unconscious. It would have looked like a random mugging had it not been for the fact that my father's head of security had received reports about people using the summer house and chose that afternoon to check it out for himself. He arrived as they were leaving. They were arrested and I was flown to hospital.'

'How seriously were you hurt?'

'Four broken ribs, ruptured spleen, two broken fingers on my left hand. The scar you saw on my back was where he dragged me over a gravel path.'

'So that's why you box. And why you don't have bodyguards.'

'I do, sometimes, but these days I prefer to be responsible for my own security.'

Izzy burned with outrage. 'I hope she gets wrinkles and has a horrid life.'

'She did me a favour.' His face was expressionless. 'Because of her I learned not to let myself get close to anyone. I realised that women were attracted to my title and position, not me. Maybe not all of them—' he gave a humourless smile '—but I learned that it was impossible to judge. It was the last time I allowed myself to trust anyone.'

And now she understood why he'd behaved the way he had towards her. 'Right from the start you thought I'd be bad for the royal family. You thought I'd damage your reputation or try and squeeze money out of you.'

He breathed deeply. 'Yes to all that.'

Izzy bit her lip, comforted by his honesty even though it was painful to hear. 'You loved her, didn't you?'

'I thought I did.'

'I did a search on you. Why is there nothing about this on the internet?'

'My father has had decades of experience of handling delicate situations. Only a couple of people knew the truth. The press were told I'd come off my motorbike.' His laugh was bitter. 'An excuse I objected to strongly because I have never had an accident in my life.'

'And what happened to the film?'

'It was destroyed. Carly was so panicked by how out of control her brother had been, she handed it over in return for a reduced sentence.'

Izzy hesitated. 'I'm glad you told me. I wish you'd told me sooner.'

'The surprise is that I've told you now.' His expression was guarded and she realised that he was absorbing the enormity of what he'd done.

'No big deal,' she said quickly. 'I never gossip.' But the fact that he *had* told her warmed her.

Made her feel special. 'So you lay in hospital for weeks.'

'Bored out of my mind. Bitter. Angry. I stayed that way until a very long-suffering nurse became fed up with my complaining, wrestled me into a wheelchair and took me up to the children's ward. They were rushed off their feet and they needed someone to read to a little girl who had no visitors.' His voice softened. 'That's how it started.'

'How what started?'

'The Prince's Fund. That nurse was clever and she did me a bigger favour than Carly because she made sure I saw how lucky I was. I deserved a slap, but what she gave me was insight. In those weeks after the accident I saw a world I hadn't seen before. I saw children who smiled even though they were sick. I saw parents in desperate financial straits make every sacrifice to get the best possible care for their children. I saw life in the raw. It wasn't Carly who changed my life, it was the time I spent in hospital. Before that, I hadn't really known what to do with myself. I was the second son. The spare to the heir. The understudy. And then I realised that I could use that influence for good. By the time I was discharged I knew what my role was going to be.'

There was a lump in her throat. 'And you've been doing it ever since.'

'I discovered that my name and my presence at events attracted big money and I took that money and ploughed it back into my charity.'

She rubbed her toe on the floor. 'For what it's worth, I know how it feels to discover someone was just using you, so I sympathise.'

'Is this the point where we talk about Brian?'

'Please, let's not.'

'I'm surprised you didn't punch him for leaving you at the altar.'

'I didn't want him to think I cared enough to punch him. I danced until four in the morning and ended up kissing a total stranger in the hope that it would get into the papers and show him I didn't care. Of course that was the only picture the press never took—' she shrugged '—so I kissed some vile slobbery guy for no reason. What happened after Carly? I know you started the charity, but what about your own relationships?'

'I'm not good at relationships.'

'I read that about you. Mr Heartbreaker. And then you discovered that your brother was marrying a Jackson and you thought, *Here we go again. These people are the worst kind of trou-*

ble.' Seeing the wary look in his eyes, Izzy managed a smile. 'It's OK. I'd rather you were honest and it's a natural reaction. We all judge from the outside to some extent. I thought you were an arrogant prince who was full of himself.'

'*The me you don't see.*'

'Exactly.'

He didn't smile. 'It is very much on my conscience that I was so vile to you. You should have been crushed by what I said and it's a reflection of your strength and determination that you brushed yourself off and carried on trying. I have never met anyone more tenacious than you.'

'Tenacious, as in pushy?'

'Tenacious as in focused.' His hand curved behind her head and he drew her towards him. 'It was your focus that kept us from doing something foolish last night, not my self-control. I'm grateful for that.'

Izzy's heart was pounding. 'I like the fact you lost control. It was sort of a compliment.'

Part of her was desperately hoping he'd continue where they'd left off but she sensed his withdrawal and she could have screamed at the irony because she understood that the very confession which should have deepened the intimacy between them had caused him to back off.

He'd taken a step he hadn't taken before and he wasn't comfortable with it.

There was a tense silence and then his eyes narrowed thoughtfully. 'I need to take a shower. Meet me at the recording studio in twenty minutes and bring all those notebooks. Everything you've ever written. And start warming up your voice.'

'Why?'

'We're going to do something about those goals of yours. It's time to record your songs.'

In a state of conflict and not enjoying the sensation one little bit, Matteo watched Izzy in the vocal booth. He was all too aware that his inexplicable loss of control the night before had been compounded by an even greater lapse when he'd revealed information that was both confidential and deeply personal. Even had he been able to explain away the first as the natural response of a male with a healthy sex drive, nothing explained the second. Since when had he felt the need to serve up the truth about his past for public consumption? The moment he'd launched into his confession he'd wanted to withdraw the words but it had been too late for that and the realisation that he'd spilled his darkest secret to someone he barely knew filled him with cold panic.

Sharing secrets was the first step to intimacy and he avoided emotional intimacy at all costs. He was a master at keeping women at a distance. He prided himself on the wall of protection he'd constructed around himself. And yet somehow Izzy, through a lethal mixture of natural charm and sheer perseverance, had managed to find a weakness. And that perseverance shouldn't have surprised him because it was her trademark. He could see it now as she sang. If something wasn't right, she did it again. And again, until she was satisfied it was the best it could be.

He'd never known anyone work so hard.

'She's incredible.' Even Phil, his engineer producer who had seen it all before and was never complimentary about anyone, was impressed.

They worked for nine hours straight, nine hours during which Matteo brooded and simmered. By the end of it she was still buzzing with energy.

'That was so cool. Thank you.' Virtually dancing on the spot, she gave Phil a huge kiss. 'I will love you forever.'

Seriously unsettled by how much that innocent

kiss bothered him, Matteo propelled Izzy out of the door with undignified haste and she looked at him in astonishment.

'What's the hurry?'

'I assumed you were hungry.' He was *not* jealous, he told himself. It would be irrational to be jealous and he was never irrational. 'We missed breakfast and lunch. I've organized food.'

'You mean you gave an order and fifty staff jumped into action.'

No one else dared to speak to him the way she did and it shook him because teasing was another dangerous step towards intimacy and he had no intention of going down that path.

As she noticed the rug spread out on the grass next to the fountain, she stopped dead. Her eyes settled on the champagne in the ice bucket and Matteo had to concede that his staff had risen to the challenge of recreating fine dining outdoors.

He watched, fascinated by the delight that spread across her pretty face, and then tensed as she flung her arms round him.

'Oh, *thank* you! This is perfect.'

The spontaneous display of affection caught him off guard. 'It's just a picnic. Not a Michelin-starred restaurant.'

'But that's just it—' her voice was husky '—you knew I'd hate a Michelin-starred restaurant because I bet they have a confusing amount of forks. This is so much more romantic. Wow.'

Romantic?

He'd instructed his team to provide food outside. He hadn't said anything about romantic. He'd prepared an evening he thought she might enjoy and the fact that she'd loaded the gesture with additional meaning sent him into rapid reverse. 'I'd offer you champagne,' he said smoothly, extracting himself from her hug, 'but after seeing the effect it had on you the night of the party I'm not sure I'm ready to take that risk.'

His sudden withdrawal earned him a puzzled look. Then she smiled. 'But this time you're feeding me.' She knelt down on the rug. 'I bet your staff died of shock when you said you wanted to eat outside.'

'They died of shock when I carried you upstairs to bed on the first night. Since then it has sadly become a common occurrence to see me behaving oddly.' *And if they could read his mind their shock would treble.*

'It isn't odd, it's normal.' Picking up a fork, she

helped herself to chicken. 'You should relax more often.'

Having just made a conscious decision that he needed to relax *less* in her company, Matteo swiftly changed the subject. 'Tell me more about your singing. Why did no one in your family encourage you?'

'No one in my family is remotely interested in music.'

'That's why you entered *Singing Star*.'

'It seemed like a great idea. I was seventeen.' She gave a wry smile. 'It seems as though we both made our formative mistakes in our teens.'

The brief reminder of his earlier confession was like a shower of cold water.

'We were talking about you,' Matteo said hastily, and she glanced at him briefly and then gave a shrug.

'I naively thought they'd hear my voice and that would be it. Of course it was nothing like that. They weren't interested in the voice, just the package and the fact that I was hopeless at hiding my feelings. There was so much footage of "Izzy losing it," they didn't know which bit to use next. There were a few grumblings in the press about me being exploited, but mostly people just thought

I was awful and deserved everything bad that happened to me.' Her light tone didn't cover the hurt and Matteo felt a rush of cold anger towards the people who had used her in such an unethical way.

'Where were your parents when this happened?'

'Chantelle believes in letting a person make her own mistakes. And as for Dad—he loves us all but he's very selfish and spends most of his time—'

'Spends most of his time—?'

Izzy stabbed a piece of chicken with her fork, her cheeks pinker than before. 'Having sex with his ex-wife. You can't possibly be interested in all this. Can I eat this with my fingers or is that bad manners?'

Matteo discovered that he was interested in everything about her. 'You can eat it in any way you wish. He still sleeps with his ex-wife?' He felt genuinely horrified for her. 'How does your mother cope with that?'

'As long as she has the status of being his wife, that's all she minds about.' Izzy put her plate down, the rest of the food untouched. 'And I hate that. That's not love. That's a business arrangement. I don't ever want that. I had a narrow escape with Brian. That's why I'm no good at relation-ships. Since then I've just avoided all that emo-tional stuff.'

'Good decision.' Relieved by that declaration, Matteo sprang to his feet. 'And if there is one thing guaranteed to take your mind off emotional mess, it's physical activity. I can recommend it.'

Her eyes widened. 'What sort of physical activ-ity did you have in mind?'

'Swimming,' he purred, 'what else? Are you wearing a bikini?'

Those blue eyes dropped to his mouth. 'Yes, but it's miles to the swimming pool from here.'

'Who said anything about a swimming pool?' Deciding that if he didn't get her in cold water soon they'd both be in serious trouble, Matteo hauled her to her feet, closed his hands round the hem of her dress and lifted it over her head. Underneath she was wearing a minuscule tur-quoise bikini that revealed more than it concealed and he felt raw lust slam into him.

'When did you get that tattoo?'

Her eyes twinkled naughtily. 'The day Chantelle said, "Whatever you do, don't get a tattoo." What's a girl supposed to do? I wasn't an easy teenager. You should probably feel sorry for her.'

'I don't.' Matteo found it impossible to feel sorry for a woman who had clearly given her daughter so little support. Stripping to his swimming shorts, he scooped her into his arms.

Izzy squealed with shock. 'Don't you dare drop me in the water. Don't you—agh—' Her words gurgled as Matteo dropped her into the water beneath the fountain and when she surfaced she came up spluttering and swinging for him.

She was wet and slippery but he caught her easily and took her down again and this time he went with her into the cool water.

'I can't believe you're swimming in your fountain!' Gasping and laughing, she gave him a shove. 'There's hope for you yet, Your Highness.'

'Stop calling me Your Highness.'

'You told me that was the correct mode of address.'

'The first time.' He slid his hand behind her neck and drew her face to his, reminding himself that physical intimacy was completely different from emotional intimacy. 'We've gone way past that.' Devouring her mouth in a hot kiss, he backed her out of the water. Still kissing they stumbled over the edge of the fountain, paused long enough to scoop up the blanket and their clothes and then he swung her into his arms again and strode towards the maze.

This type of intimacy held no fear for him whatsoever.

CHAPTER EIGHT

THE maze was a mysterious world of sunlight and dappled shade, the tall hedges giving each path its own feeling of privacy.

Quivering with anticipation, Izzy wrapped her arms around him. 'Why here?'

'Because it's closer than the palazzo.'

'Well, don't lose me—' she buried her face in his neck '—I have a hopeless sense of direction. My body won't be discovered for at least a decade.'

'Your body is going to be discovered a lot sooner than that.' Matteo strode purposefully along a path, took a left then a right and flung down his shirt and the towels in the little clearing. Then he gently lowered her to the ground and brought his mouth down on hers.

Izzy's resistance melted like ice in a heatwave. All the sensations from the night before came rushing back. It was as if they'd never stopped.

As if the time in between had been nothing more than a pause.

His hands were hard on her shoulders, his mouth warm and seductive, and she slid down into the dark, erotic depths of his kiss.

'I've never met a woman who makes me feel the way you do.' He muttered the words against her lips. 'It drives me mad.'

'Me too.' Izzy gave a soft whimper as his mouth trailed down her neck. 'Don't stop.'

'I want you so badly I can't even make it back to the palazzo.'

It was some consolation that he felt that way too. But even through the lethal buzz of sexual chemistry, part of her refused to completely abdicate her responsibilities.

'Do you have—?'

'Yes. I'm not making that mistake twice.' His fingers smoothed her damp skin and she shivered with anticipation as she felt his hand on her thigh.

'There's something I need to say to you.' Her tone was urgent. 'I'm nothing like Carly.'

He inhaled sharply. 'Izzy—'

'I just want you to know that I'd never—'

He silenced her with a hot, hard kiss. 'You

think I'd be here with you if I thought you were like her?'

'For what it's worth, I didn't plan any of this to happen.' It seemed imperative that he know that and he paused. His head blocked the sun and she stared into the raw hunger in his eyes, feeling something she'd never felt before.

'Neither did I.' With unsteady fingers he removed her bikini top. 'I didn't plan this either. The intention was to haul you off that stage and keep you out of trouble. But you've been nothing but trouble from the moment I put you in my car. I can't believe what you do to me. You drive me crazy.'

Izzy was about to say that he had the same effect on her when his mouth brushed against her nipple and sensation shot through her body like a lightning bolt. She squirmed, consumed by a fiery flash of heat that burned from head to toe. Realising that the power was all his, she gave a moan of desperation and slid her leg over his, locking him against her.

His mouth returned to hers, hot and demanding. She felt the erotic slide of his tongue, the scrape of male stubble against her cheek and the sure touch of his hands on her body, and the world around her ceased to exist. She was aware of nothing except him, not the heat of the sun pounding down on them, the stillness of the hot summer air or the occasional rustle of leaves in the shadows of the maze. Her world was reduced to just this man and the sensations that engulfed her.

Sure and confident, he kissed his way down her body, driving her wild with the skill of his mouth and the touch of his hands. And she touched back, her hands as bold as his, as urgent for him as he was for her.

At some point—she wasn't even sure when—she lost the rest of her bikini and he spread her thighs with possessive hands and subjected her to an exploration of such intimacy that her body caught fire.

'Matteo…' She moaned his name and he responded by shifting her under the virile heat of his body.

Their mouths clashed and this time the kiss was crazy, hot and out of control. Dimly, she was aware of him dragging something from his abandoned shirt and then of the brief pause during which she thought her body was going to explode from sheer desperation. She felt the hardness of him against her and had no time to even gasp before he was surging into her, each rhythmic thrust taking him deeper, joining them completely, and it felt so impossibly good that she cried out his name and arched into him. Sensation robbed her of breath. There were things she wanted to say but she couldn't form the words so she just closed her eyes and gave herself up to the moment.

And he knew what he wanted and he took it, took *her* as she lay beneath him on the grassy track with the sun dappling the earth around them. But she was past caring about her surroundings and so was he and she slid her hands into his hair instinctively, trying to hold on to something solid as her body flew into the storm. He kissed through all of it, held her as her body splintered around his, as each spasm that ripped through her ripped through him until her body robbed his of control.

Weakened by a sheer overload of sensation, Izzy lay beneath him, limp and in shock.

Gradually the world intruded. She became aware of the sweet notes of birdsong, of the hard ground pressing through the thin layer of the towel and of his body, sleek and powerful, still covering hers. And she became aware of the pounding of her own heart and feelings that were new to her. Strong feelings.

'Matt...' Some of those feelings seeped into the way she said his name and she instantly regretted that lapse because she felt him tense and knew she'd shattered the moment.

The hand that had been stroking her hair stilled.

When he lifted his head and looked down at her his eyes were veiled.

'We should probably move,' he said in a neutral tone. 'This place is secluded but not exactly secret.'

The sudden thud of disappointment made no sense because a man like him, who had avoided emotional commitment and intimacy for his entire life, wasn't suddenly going to embrace it after one hot encounter, was he?

Even so, as he sprang to his feet she wanted to drag him back to her, to prolong the moment because it had felt so real, and for that little sliver of time she'd wanted to pretend it was something different.

But the moment had passed and he was the prince again.

He didn't need bodyguards, Izzy thought

numbly, because he'd built a steel cage around himself.

But at least he hadn't lied to her, she reminded herself as she reached for her bikini. What they'd shared had been honest. He'd made no promises and neither had she. For a moment she thought about Brian and then pushed the thought away. No way was she letting Brian ruin this moment.

Feeling his gaze on her, Izzy slithered back into her bikini and forced herself to be matter-of-fact. 'Nice…maze.'

A reluctant smile tugged at the corners of his mouth as he dressed swiftly. 'It has never been used for that purpose before. We should go.'

So that was that then.

A one-night stand. Probably something neither of them would speak of again.

Pondering on the practicalities of outdoor sex, Izzy extracted a leaf from her hair. 'I expect you want to go back separately.'

He frowned. 'What would be the point of that?'

'I thought you were worried about shocking your staff.'

'My staff can mind their own business. I refuse to creep around my own palazzo and it would be absurd to leave separately when we're both going to end up in the same place. My bedroom.'

'Your...bedroom?'

'You thought we were going to spend the night in the maze?'

'No! I thought— Never mind.' The smile spread right through her as she realised that this wasn't over yet. 'So what happens now?'

'You pick up your shoes,' he drawled, yanking her against him and lowering his mouth to hers. 'That's assuming you don't want to break with tradition and put them on your feet.'

Two weeks later Izzy lay on her stomach on Matteo's office floor, papers spread out in front of her as she poured over the lyrics for her latest song. It was past midnight and she'd been working since daybreak. Her shoes were abandoned on the floor next to her, along with three empty coffee mugs and the remains of a hastily eaten lunch. 'I'm excited about this one.'

Matteo lifted his gaze from the computer. 'You should take a break. You've been working on that all day.'

Izzy sat up and stretched out her aching muscles. 'I don't see you taking one.'

'I'm responsible for the success of the concert.'

Looking at him, her stomach flipped. He was *so* sexy. Every time he walked into the room her knees wobbled. They'd spent two weeks together, recording music, planning the last details of the concert, and she'd been in the thick of it and loving every minute. And when they weren't working they were having sex. Often and everywhere. In his bedroom, in the maze and on the small private beach that nestled at the bottom of the cliffs that guarded the palazzo. And although she knew that for him their relationship was just physical, for her it had become so much more. But after that first time Izzy had been supremely careful not to even hint at an emotional connection.

'I heard your demo today.' He leaned back in his chair, the movement drawing attention to the width of his shoulders. 'It's genius. You should have sung your own material on *Singing Star.*'

'They wouldn't let me.' Izzy glowed. After a decade of being dismissed and diminished at every turn, suddenly she was being appreciated and the high that came from that was something she hadn't been able to imagine. And if that high was slightly tainted by the fact that he showed no inclination to deepen their personal relationship then she tried to ignore it. 'I still can't believe my record went straight to number one or that it's only two nights until the actual concert.'

'That record is a major hit, *tesoro*.'

'Unbelievable.' Izzy sat watching him as he finished entering a stack of numbers onto a spreadsheet. 'You have no idea what these past few weeks have been like for me. No one has ever asked my opinion on anything before,' she said humbly. 'I'm used to hearing, "Shut up, Izzy."' The fact that he encouraged her to sing at every opportunity made her feel warm inside. And as for the rest of it…

Her eyes met his and she blushed because looking at him always did wild, crazy things to her insides.

'We're going to celebrate.' He rose to his feet. 'Tomorrow I'm taking you back to the palace.'

Izzy's heart lifted and flew. He was going to introduce her properly to his parents? 'Really?'

'It's the Annual Rock 'n' Royal Ball. A fund-raising event that takes place every year the night before the concert. You're coming as my guest.'

So their celebration wasn't going to be an intimate evening but a huge, glittering event. Panic set in. 'It's a big formal thing?'

'If you're worrying about which knife and fork to use then don't. You're going to be fine. Just be yourself and everyone will love you.'

Izzy doubted that. People didn't usually even like her, let alone love her. They sneered and made disparaging comments, and now that she understood just how much the reputation of the royal family mattered to him, she didn't want him tainted with that. 'I don't think it would be a great idea. Everyone would just laugh at me.'

Her comment drew a frown from him. 'Why would they laugh at you?'

'Because that's what they do.'

'If I see anyone so much as smile at you in a way that doesn't please me I will knock them into next week.'

'And how would that help? You don't need the adverse publicity just before the concert.' And just thinking of that reminded her of how utterly impossible their relationship was. Even if she managed to wriggle through the protective force field he'd spun around himself there was still the fact that he was a prince to contend with. Her mood plummeted. 'And neither do Allegra and Alex.'

'Stop worrying.' Dismissing her fears, he glanced at his watch. 'We'll leave first thing tomorrow so you can pack tonight. I have to talk to Serena about a couple of things.'

Pack what? A red sequin dress that had made her the focus of mockery? A fuchsia bikini?

She knew nothing about dressing for a formal event, but she did know that there wasn't a thing in her wardrobe that was suitable.

'What time is our flight?'

He paused on his way out of the door. 'Whenever I decide it is. It's my plane.'

And that comment only highlighted the difference between them. 'I've never raised money for anyone. I have no idea what to say or do and I don't want to mess it up.' *Nor did she want to wear the wrong thing.*

Suddenly she wished she'd paid better attention to what the other women were wearing at the engagement party.

She was not going to give anyone reason to gossip or say bad things about her.

Matteo was looking at her in genuine astonishment. 'It's just a ball. Enjoy yourself. And afterwards there's somewhere I want to take you so pack your red sequin dress for later.' Having issued that instruction he walked out of his office to talk to Serena, and Izzy watched him with a sick feeling in her stomach.

Why would he want her to pack her sequin dress 'for later'?

Were they going dancing or something?

Or maybe that was his way of tactfully telling her it wasn't suitable for the main event.

Thinking fast, she pulled her notebook out of her bag and made a list. The moment Matteo went off to take a call she shot in to see Serena. 'You're one of those PAs who can do anything, aren't you?' Her face scarlet, Izzy slapped a list down on her desk. 'Any chance you could get me copies of those magazines?'

Serena scanned the list. If she was surprised, she didn't show it. 'No problem.'

'And do you happen to know good places to shop? Nothing too expensive but it has to look as if it costs a fortune and absolutely no one else can be wearing it.'

Serena's eyes widened in surprise and then she gave a warm smile. 'I know the perfect place. I'll ask Matteo's driver to take you there. But I'm sure if you mentioned it to Matteo, he'd—'

'No thanks,' Izzy said fiercely, 'I can buy it myself but I don't know *what* to buy and that's why

I need all those magazines. I have some serious homework to do.'

Serena glanced at the list. 'Homework? I assumed you were just a lover of women's fashion magazines.'

'I need to see how other people look.' Izzy fumbled in her bag and put some money on the desk. 'That should cover it. And now I have to go and work. My Goal of the Day is to make myself stylish. I have a feeling it's going to take some work.'

Twenty-four hours later Matteo paced the length of his private apartment at the palace for the tenth time and glanced impatiently towards the closed door of the master bedroom.

What could be taking her so long?

If she didn't get a move on, the guests would be greeting themselves.

How long did it take one woman to pull on a dress?

Accustomed to women whose life objective appeared to be gaining access to his credit card, it had come as a surprise when Izzy had refused to let him fund her shopping trip. Even when he'd pointed out that he was the reason she needed to go shopping, she'd shaken her head.

As someone who was rigidly punctual, Matteo was about to stride into the bedroom and dress her himself when the door opened slowly.

'Sorry I took so long. I've never tried to pin my hair up before. It kept falling down and then I couldn't see what the back looked like. Complete nightmare.' She reminded him of a doe emerging from the cover of trees, waiting to be eaten.

She looked stunning, but it wasn't her appearance that knocked him off balance; it was his reaction to her obvious vulnerability. Discovering a powerful protective streak he hadn't known he possessed, Matteo tensed. 'We should go. We are *extremely* late.'

'You're telling me I look awful.' Her face fell and the exasperation he felt towards his own reaction somehow became directed at her.

'No, I'm telling you we're going to be late!'

'But you're *thinking* I look awful.'

Matteo breathed deeply. What he was actually thinking was that if there was one thing all women had in common it was an obsessive wish to dissect the contents of a man's mind. 'I'm not thinking anything except how to get you downstairs quickly,' he lied. 'Here's an insider tip—if a man tells you he's thinking nothing then he's genuinely thinking nothing. Men are not like women.'

'And here's another insider tip—' her voice was high-pitched '—when a woman has spent two hours getting ready for an event she's dreading it's a good idea to say something positive!'

Matteo stilled. 'You're dreading it?'

'I already *told* you that.'

'Then why are you doing it?'

'Because you asked me to! Now can we just go and get it over with?'

Because you asked me to.

Trying not to think about what emotion might drive someone to make that sacrifice, he made a belated attempt to smooth things over. 'You look *stunning.*'

'Too late. A compliment is meaningless if you have to be tortured before you say it.' Without looking at him, she stalked towards the door.

'You are completely overreacting!' But he knew that he was entirely responsible for the sudden tension between them and the guilt intensified his dark mood. Trying to redeem the situation before a private disagreement became a public one, Matteo scanned the elegant cobalt sheath that curved into her waist and flared at the floor.

'Truly, the dress is perfect, *tesoro*. Obviously you had a highly successful shopping trip.'

'Actually, it wasn't that successful. I started off in a couple of designer stores, but I have boobs and a bum which makes it hard to find anything that looks good.' Her knuckles were white as she clutched her purse tightly. 'A sales assistant told me in a very snooty voice that all the designer dresses look best on women whose bodies don't interrupt the flow of the clothes. Evidently that's not me. It feels nice on, but it isn't by anyone famous or anything so doubtless there will be some fun headlines about that tomorrow. Can we just go? Honestly, the anticipation is worse than the reality, or at least I hope it is.'

Matteo realised just how much he was asking of her, inviting her as his guest to such a high-profile function.

'Izzy—'

'Please don't say anything else.' She pulled open the door and stalked out of the apartment even though she had no idea where she was going. 'Let's just get through this.'

Accustomed to women who thrived on events like this one, Matteo made a rapid adjustment and steered her towards a private elevator.

As the doors closed, offering them privacy, he reached into his pocket. 'This is for you.'

She stared at the slim box in his hand. 'So now you're trying to buy your way out of trouble?'

'I bought this *before* I got myself into trouble,' he drawled. 'It's a gift.'

'Why would you buy me a gift?'

Already struggling with his own behaviour, Matteo decided he didn't want to think about why. Instead he flipped open the box. 'I hope you like it.'

She gasped. 'Oh—'

'It's a daisy chain. The petals are platinum and the centres are diamonds. Hopefully it will last longer than the real thing.'

She didn't speak and he frowned.

'*Now* what's wrong?'

'You had this in your pocket the whole time?'

'Yes. I intended to give it to you earlier but you took a long time to get ready, which is fine,' Matteo said hastily, intercepting her warning glance, 'because the end result was definitely worth the wait. You really are stunning.'

'You chose this for me and it's the most perfect thing anyone has ever given me. And I've been so snappy,' she wailed. 'I'm sorry.'

'*Don't* apologise for something that was my fault.' Seeing the sheen of tears in her eyes, Matteo felt a flash of panic. Focusing on the practical, he fastened the necklace and then the matching bracelet. 'It looks pretty on you. Do you like it?'

'*Love.*' She touched her throat. 'Love, not like.'

Matteo had never found the elevator so stuffy. 'It's a congratulations present,' he said smoothly, 'and a thank-you for the work you did on the song.'

Her gaze held his for a moment and then she gave a wry smile. 'Chill, Your Highness. It's the necklace I love, not you. Shall we go?'

CHAPTER NINE

IT WAS like trying to tame a tiger.

He'd existed on his own for so long that even the thought of allowing someone close made him dangerous.

He'd given her a stunning present and then proceeded to virtually bolt from the elevator to escape her thanks. He was programmed to respond to the word *love* the way most people respond to *fire*. Alarms went off around him and evoked an immediate evacuation of the area.

Her brain ached with the complexity of handling their relationship.

And as if she didn't have enough to think about, now she was expected to pose for photographs on the steps of the palace before the ball started.

'Paparazzi photo call,' she quipped, 'otherwise known as feeding time at the zoo.'

He shot her a warning glance as the doors were opened. 'Don't speak. They can read lips.'

Izzy pinned a smile on her face and hoped they

couldn't read minds or the headlines were going to be interesting.

They stepped onto the steps at the front of the palace and Matteo closed his hand over hers as what felt like a million flashlights exploded.

'Smile,' he ordered in an undertone, so she dutifully smiled and gripped his hand so hard she was sure he'd have permanent indentations from the pressure of her nails on his flesh. And tonight he was very much the prince, cool and in control as he fielded the hoard of paparazzi and public eager for a glimpse of him.

Once inside, he drew her towards a line of people waiting to meet him.

'They want to meet you, not me,' Izzy muttered, but he propelled her forward, refusing to let her hide.

For the next hour she had no time to think about anything as she shook a million hands and said, 'So pleased to meet you,' again and again until finally they moved into the ballroom with its ornate ceiling and crystal chandeliers. Giant screens at the side of the stage were playing footage of previous Rock 'n' Royal concerts and Izzy's heart sank as she discovered that she was seated next to one of Matteo's most important guests, a sheikh.

Daunted by his severe expression but even more daunted by the prospect of an awkward silence, Izzy frantically searched her brain for something interesting to say that didn't include the weather.

'Do you know that camels are the only animal whose red blood cells are shaped like a sphere?'

The sheikh appeared startled by the question. 'I did not know that.'

'It's to do with them getting dehydrated.' Izzy picked up her fork but knew she wasn't going to be able to eat a thing. She was too nervous. 'The red blood cells don't clump together. I find that fascinating...' Realising that he was staring at her in astonishment her voice trailed off. 'But I realise that most people don't so maybe we should just talk about something else. The weather maybe...' She was about to slide under the table when he smiled and that smile was surprisingly warm.

'I find it fascinating too. Are you an expert in veterinary science?'

'No. I'm not an expert in anything. But I did a project on camels at school.' Grateful to him for being so nice, Izzy gave up on the food on her plate. 'I think they start at a disadvantage because they're noisy and smelly on the outside. And what you see on the outside isn't always a reflection of what's on the inside, is it?'

'It is not. I am in complete agreement. If only more people remembered that, the world would indeed be a better place.' The sheikh reached for his glass, and as he started to tell her more about his home and his family, she realised that however important he was, in the end he was just a person with hopes and insecurities like everyone else.

The me you don't see.

Across the table her eyes met Matteo's.

Despite everything they'd shared, he hadn't lowered his guard. The emotional distance was still there. And she was starting to think it always would be.

Half wishing she could meet Carly so that she could punch her on the nose, Izzy carried on her conversation with the sheikh and enjoyed his company so much that she barely noticed the time passing until she heard the notes of her song playing and saw the music video playing on the big screen.

Her song.

Matteo raised his glass in a silent toast and as soon as the song ended he rose to his feet and silence fell across the packed ballroom, as if someone had hit a switch and turned off the sound.

He spoke eloquently, without the help of notes, highlighting the various charities that had been supported by the Prince's Fund.

He wore his fame and status lightly, she thought. Yes, he used it when it suited him and then he set it aside. It was just another weapon in his impressive armoury and yet another thing that made her melt inside. She admired him so much.

Who was she kidding? What she felt was far deeper than admiration and that was what scared her.

As the auction began she sat still, careful not to move a muscle in case she accidently bid for something. But when the sheikh parted with several million dollars for the chance to mingle backstage with rock stars, she gave him a spontaneous hug and was incredibly touched when he invited her to visit his family whenever she liked.

And then the auction was over and Matteo drew her onto the dance floor.

Aware that everyone was watching, Izzy couldn't relax. 'Why is no one else dancing?'

'We open the dancing. It's tradition. How was your dinner?'

'I have no idea. I felt too sick to eat it. Why did you sit me next to someone as important as the sheikh?'

'Because I knew he'd like you. You're unusual.'

'Thanks.'

'It was a compliment,' he murmured as he pulled her closer. 'You're not daunted by wealth or power.'

'I was definitely daunted! I was so daunted I couldn't eat! And if I've caused a diplomatic incident it's your fault.'

'He was thoroughly charmed, as I knew he would be.'

Izzy relented. 'He's a nice man actually. And he owns an awful lot of camels. Which he probably can no longer afford to feed now he's donated so much to your charity, *not* that I'm saying it isn't a worthy cause—'

'I wouldn't worry too much about the welfare of those camels,' Matteo drawled, pulling her against him. 'He owns most of a desert and several oil fields.' His hand was warm and strong against her bare back and as the heat rose between them he breathed deeply and eased her away from him. 'Time to go.'

'You can't leave yet.'

'I can do anything I like. It's my party.' His mouth flickered at the corners. 'And besides, there is somewhere I want to take you. Did you bring that dress with the sequins?'

'Yes, but—'

'*Bene*. Let's fetch it from the apartment and then go.'

She'd been expecting a nightclub, but instead he took her to the huge hospital, a contemporary building with views of the sea.

Walking in through a rear entrance, clearly familiar with the layout, the prince took a flight of stairs and buzzed the door of the children's unit.

A brisk, efficient-looking woman opened the door and let them in.

'We weren't expecting you tonight!' She beamed at Matteo, clearly delighted to see him. 'We assumed you'd be too tired from the effort of parting people from their money.'

'Raised twice as much as last year.' Without releasing Izzy's hand, Matteo strode onto the ward. 'Where are they all?'

'You really need to ask? In the den, as always. You should know, you paid for it. They were all in there earlier, watching you on the news as you walked down the red carpet.' Her voice softened and she gave Izzy a warm smile. 'I can't believe you came. Thank you! Your Royal Highness, when you've said hello, why don't you and your guest pop in and see Jessica? She's had a rough day and this will lift her spirits.'

Matteo nodded. 'That's why we came.'

The den turned out to be a large, airy room equipped with sofas, bean bags and enough electronic equipment to satisfy the most demanding teenager.

Izzy looked around her and thought about the fact that a visit from the prince could make someone's day. Only now was it dawning on her just what an impact he had on people. 'You paid for this?'

'The Prince's Fund supports the hospital, among other things. There was the need for a specialist teenage unit. We provided the funding to equip the place.' He lifted his hand to his throat and undid his bow tie with a few deft flicks of his fingers. Two teenage boys and a girl were playing pool in one corner, but the moment they spotted Matt, they stopped.

'Hey!' The girl grinned and rested her hand on her hip. 'Looking hot, Your Highness.'

'Behave yourself.' But Matt was smiling as he strolled across to talk to the three young people.

Izzy couldn't hear what he said but whatever it was had them all laughing.

Looking round, she noticed that one wall was dominated by a huge flat-screen TV and next to it a library of DVDs and computer games. In the corner was a kitchen complete with popcorn maker.

'Izzy?' Matteo took her hand and led her towards a two-bedded room. 'I want you to meet someone. This is Jessica.'

Izzy looked at the pale face of the girl on the bed. 'Hi—' she gave an awkward smile '—ignore me. I'm just a hanger-on. Honestly, you just go ahead and talk to Matteo and pretend I'm not here.'

'Pretend you're not—' The girl gave an excited gasp and turned to Matteo. 'You brought her! Thank you—you said you would but I didn't believe you.' She turned back to Izzy, her eyes filling with tears. 'You're, like, *totally* my hero. I love you so much. We all do.'

Izzy stared at her. 'You love *me*?'

'I've got all your songs on my iPod,' Jessica burst out, 'you're my inspiration. Will you sign something? If I'd known you were coming I would have asked my mum to bring in the poster I have of you.'

Overwhelmed and feeling decidedly undeserving, Izzy fiddled with a strand of her hair. 'You're mixing me up with someone. My last single bombed. I mess up quite often.'

'I know. But you never give up. You get knocked down and then you pick yourself up again. Even when you make mistakes, you keep going—' Jessica's eyes shone '—and when I saw those pictures of you crying in your wedding dress...'

Izzy pulled a face. 'You saw those?'

'Yes, and the ones when you kissed that guy and you were, like, "I am *not* going to let a man ruin my life," and then you went to all those parties even though you were *totally* miserable—'

'I looked miserable?'

'Yes, but the thing is, you didn't just lie down and pull the covers over your head. Loads of people would have given up, but you didn't. Would you sign this for me?' Jessica scrabbled in the locker by her bed and dragged out a stack of magazines, all open to articles on Izzy. 'You're so brave. And you look amazing. Mum says that once I'm better she's going to try and find me a red sequin dress like the one you wore to the engagement party at the palace. I've got a picture of it right here.'

'You liked that dress?'

'Ohmigod, are you kidding? It totally rocks.'

Suddenly Izzy understood why Matteo had wanted her to bring the dress. She looked at the girl's pale face and pulled it out of the bag. 'Here—you might have to have it taken in a bit because I'm much bigger than you.' She pushed it into Jessica's hands. 'I'm not giving you the shoes because frankly they should come with a health warning.'

'You're giving me your dress?' Jessica held it reverentially, touching the sequins in fascination. 'You can't do that.'

'I can.' And she discovered that the delight on the girl's face gave her the same high as singing to thousands of people. 'It's yours. You'll look great in it.'

'I've never owned anything so pretty.' Jessica looked up at Matt, adoration on her face. 'I can't believe you brought her. Thank you.'

'Good job you mentioned she was your idol.' Matteo sprawled in a chair by the bed, taking a backseat as the girl questioned Izzy on everything from singing to make-up. After about twenty minutes Izzy realised he'd fallen asleep.

'He's been working hard,' she said by way of apology, and Jessica smiled.

'I don't care. It's you I wanted to see. Not that I'm saying he's not cool, because he is. He raises loads and loads of money and he's always popping in here when no one is looking. You'd think he'd want the press to know but he isn't like that.'

'No.' Izzy thought about all the times she'd courted publicity for her own sake. Matteo used who he was for the good of other people. His cold, 'moody' act was simply that. An act, to keep the wrong sort of person at a distance.

Finally she understood why his reputation mattered to him so much. It wasn't just that he wanted people to be positive about the royal family. It wasn't that he wanted to read good things about himself. He wasn't that shallow, and acknowledging that made her blush because she knew she was *exactly* that shallow. His reputation mattered because without it people wouldn't support the Prince's Fund. They wouldn't turn up to his charity functions and bid huge sums of money for deserving causes. If the press printed bad things about him it didn't just affect his reputation, it jeopardized the work he did and the lives of all the people he helped.

She loved him, she thought numbly. Really loved him.

And the realisation terrified her because their relationship was a disaster, wasn't it? He was never going to trust any woman and she couldn't live her life walking on eggshells and worrying about letting him down.

'Are you OK?' Jessica was staring at her. 'If the doctor says my blood count is OK, Matteo is going to get some of us seats at the concert in a special roped-off VIP area or something. If my mum can alter it in time I'm going to wear this dress.'

Humbled by her bravery, Izzy reminded herself that her problems were nothing in comparison. 'That's great.'

'I expect you'll be too busy to talk to me,' Jessica said casually, and Izzy leaned across the bed and hugged her, shocked by how thin the girl was and how tightly she hugged.

'I won't be too busy,' she said huskily. 'It would be great to see you there.'

'So are you and the prince—you know—like, together?'

Izzy had no idea how to answer that. What was the definition of 'together'? 'We're friends.'

Matteo was like a castle, she thought miserably. He'd built a moat round himself for protection and so far he hadn't lowered the drawbridge.

She was beginning to think he never would.

'You're unusually quiet.' Matteo shrugged off his jacket, watching Izzy as she slipped off her shoes. 'Did the visit upset you?'

'No.' She didn't look at him. 'I'm glad you took me along.'

'From the moment they saw your picture at the engagement party they've been nagging me to bring you. Especially Jessica.' Still watching her, Matteo dropped his cufflinks onto the table. 'You have a bigger fan base than you know.' Something was bothering her, that was obvious, but for once she didn't seem to be spilling her feelings all over the place.

'That's nice.'

'It was kind of you to give her the dress.' When she didn't respond he shot her a look of concern and exasperation. 'Normally I can't stop you talking. What's wrong?'

'Nothing at all.' Her smile was a little too bright. 'Unzip me?'

She turned her back and Matteo unzipped the dress.

As his hands brushed against her she turned and wrapped her arms around his neck.

'Kiss me,' she said urgently. 'Right now.'

Her head tipped back and heat went rampaging through his body. The part of him that wanted to demand to know what she was thinking was eclipsed by that primitive part of him that just wanted to flatten her to the nearest hard surface and claim her as his woman. The tangled web of contradictory messages inside himself was starting to drive him mad.

He wanted her.

But he didn't want her too close.

He was programmed to avoid intimacy but when she was the one building the barriers he just wanted to smash them down.

Losing himself in the one response he was sure of, he hauled her against him and attempted to blank out the questions in his head. Sexual excitement ripped through both of them and he felt his body harden, the arousal powerful and immediate. The unzipped dress surrendered to the firm touch of his hands and slithered to the floor. She was hot, naked and willing, and yet even in the storm of physical excitement there was no escape because he felt things he'd never felt before and wanted to say things he'd never said before.

He knew he was out of control but so was she, her nails scraping his back as he rolled her under him and entered her with a single smooth thrust that brought a gasp to her lips and a harsh exclamation to his.

'Izzy—' He closed his eyes and tried to regain some element of control but there was none to be had, not with the slick slide of her body under his and the heat of her mouth branding his throat.

Afterwards she wrapped herself around him and after a moment's hesitation he held her tightly, wondering how a hug could feel as close as a more intimate connection.

It was the closest he'd ever been to a woman and the feeling shook him so much that for hours after she'd fallen asleep he lay awake staring into the darkness.

He woke to find her already dressed in the minuscule lacy shorts that made her legs seem endless. She was stuffing clothes into her case.

Matteo sat up and ran his hand over his face. 'What are you doing?'

'Packing. The concert is tonight and I'm going home after that.'

'Home? Home as in England?'

'Where else?' Brisk and efficient, she stuffed her clothes into her case. 'And because it's going to be mad and crazy this afternoon I wanted to say thank-you now in case I don't get the chance later.'

The sudden chill in the room made him wonder if the air conditioning was malfunctioning. 'What are you thanking me for?'

'Everything you've done for my career, of course. Because of you I'm suddenly hot stuff. Well, maybe not *hot* quite yet but I'm definitely room temperature—' she pushed a bikini into a side pocket '—which is a step in the right direction after a few years in the freezer. When I made you my Goal of the Day I had no idea so much would come of it.'

Shock held him silent and then Matteo was consumed by a blast of outrage. They'd spent a month living together. They'd had the most incredible sex. *Damn it*, he'd eaten picnics and swum in his own fountain. And she was thanking him for boosting her career?

'So the past month has all been about your goal?' The hardness of his tone earned him a reproachful look.

'No, of course not! We had a lot of fun, but all good things come to an end, as they say, and you have things to do and I have things to do....'

Matteo discovered that the only thing he wanted to do was haul her back into bed and show her that some good things could be repeated as many times as necessary. 'You could stay on after the concert.'

'What would be the point of that? Neither of us has ever pretended this is anything but a fling. It was the perfect relationship. Perfect for me because I needed the boost to my confidence after that fiasco with Brian, and perfect for you because you want to keep your relationships superficial.'

Given that was indeed what he wanted, the sudden flare of his temper made no sense and the inconsistency in his own thoughts and feelings aggravated him as much as her casual dismissal of what they'd shared.

Furious with himself and with her, Matteo sprang from the bed. 'If that's what you want then

I'll arrange a flight for you immediately after the concert.'

Even that didn't earn him her full attention because she was apparently focused on trying to fasten her case. 'That's very generous of you. And thanks again for getting me a backstage pass. Wow.'

That was it?

That was all she was going to say?

Not trusting himself to speak Matteo grabbed his phone and stalked towards the bathroom. 'The concert starts at two. I need to get ready.'

Why was it that men never said what women wanted to hear?

Soaked in misery, Izzy stood in the wings watching her idols with feigned excitement, all the while thinking of nothing but Matteo.

Why, when she knew what he was like, had she expected him to argue with her when she'd reminded him he liked to keep his relationships superficial? He'd spent a lifetime avoiding intimacy so had she really believed he'd change overnight?

When he'd leapt out of the bed she'd really thought he was going to haul her into his arms and tell her not to leave, instead of which he'd strode into the shower without a backward glance in her direction.

All of which proved she'd been right in her decision to leave, but that didn't make it feel any easier.

She loved him like crazy.

Ending it had felt like cutting off part of her body and now she was bleeding inside. Maybe it wasn't so surprising that he couldn't see how she was feeling. He was so used to women who wanted him for his title and connections that it had been all too easy to convince him that she was just one more of those, especially given that her original plan had been to use him for precisely those reasons.

Surprised by how much it hurt that he could think that of her, Izzy stepped backwards as a high-profile rock band sprinted onto the stage.

She had to focus. Somehow, she had to get through the concert.

Her Goal of the Day was simply to survive and not embarrass herself.

Artist after artist performed in front of an ecstatic crowd and at one point Izzy was joined by Jessica and a few of the other teenagers from the hospital.

By the time darkness fell and they reached the climax of the concert, she was exhausted and just desperate for the whole thing to end.

Lost in her own misery, she wasn't even aware of the commotion backstage until Matteo planted himself in front of her.

Having been avoiding him all evening, Izzy flinched. 'What?'

Incredulity lit his dark eyes. 'Have you any idea what's been happening?'

Happening? 'Er, the concert is great. The audience is amazing,' she improvised, and he gritted his teeth.

'Callie has just been rushed to hospital in an ambulance.'

'Oh, dear.' Her mouth formed the words but all she could think was that she was never going to feel about anyone the way she felt about him. 'Poor her. I hope it's not serious.'

'It isn't,' he ground out, 'but what *is* serious is the fact that she's on stage next. Singing your song. You're going to have to do it.'

It took a moment for his words to sink in. 'But—'

'No one else knows it and the audience expects to hear it—it's the official song of the event. You should be pleased.' He snapped his fingers and a sound technician hurried forward with a microphone. 'This is the biggest opportunity of your life and we both know you never miss an opportunity.'

A few weeks ago she would have been on that stage faster than a cat after a mouse, but now the only thing in her head was that if her sister married his brother she'd be forced to see Matteo occasionally and that would be agony.

'I'm really not sure I can—'

'We both know you can. I'll do that.' Glowering, he snatched the microphone out of the hands of a hovering technician and fastened it himself. 'Don't even *think* about putting your hand down her T-shirt.' As the backs of his fingers brushed against her skin, Izzy shivered.

Looking at his face she thought he looked the way she felt, but then decided she was probably imagining it. Today was always going to be stressful for him. It was hardly surprising that his face was showing signs of strain.

As he drew her forward it finally sank in that she was going to have to walk onto that stage in front of a global audience of millions and sing when she was feeling horrible. Her limbs went loose and a flock of butterflies escaped in her stomach.

'I can't do this. I'm wearing shorts.'

His glance was so swift it was as if he couldn't stand the sight of her. 'You look fine, rock chick.'

'I haven't rehearsed—'

An explosion of whoops and cheers from the crowd made her jump and the next minute she was on the stage.

Oh, God...

The lights blinded her and the roar of the crowd was deafening. In the VIP area she caught a brief glimpse of Allegra with Alex and she frowned briefly because she'd had no idea they were coming.

Great. Could her humiliation be more public?

A few weeks ago she'd stood up and sung at their engagement party, ignoring the disapproving glances. Now she had an excited audience and she wasn't sure she could produce a single note.

Realising that her legs weren't going to support her, she plonked herself down at the piano and put her fingers on the keys.

An expectant hush fell over the audience and Izzy saw a beam of light track towards her.

It reminded her so much of the evening she'd

sat up in the top of the amphitheatre with Matteo that for a moment she couldn't breathe. The emotion threatened to choke her.

How could you fall in love with someone in weeks?

And how could that someone not know?

The thought that he was never going to know how she felt, that for the rest of his life he was going to think she'd just used him to fast-forward her career, made her want to sob. He was going to think she was just another of the many women who wanted something from him.

At that moment she glanced into the wings and met his gaze.

Her fingers shook on the piano keys and she stumbled once but somehow managed to struggle through the introduction to *The Me You Don't See*.

The crowd roared its approval but immediately settled as Izzy opened her mouth to sing the opening bars of the song.

'*Look at me—*' Her voice cracked with emotion and for a brief, horrible second she thought she wasn't going to be able to carry on. The only sound in her throat was a sob and she couldn't get past that because it felt wrong singing this song to a crowd of millions when it had been written for just one man.

And then she realised that this was her chance—her only chance—to tell that man how she really felt and suddenly the sob became a sound, a wonderful soaring sound as she continued. *'I'm not what you see…'* Her voice grew stronger and she forgot about the audience. Forgot about everyone and everything except the man watching her from the wings.

The man she loved.

She knew she was singing it differently from how Callie sang it, but she didn't care.

It was *her* song. This one time she was going to sing it the way she wanted to sing it—the way she'd always meant it to be sung—and she poured everything she felt into the music, and despite the huge gathering the only sound in the amphitheatre was her voice.

As the final notes died away, she dragged her gaze from Matteo and stood.

Desperate to leave, she acknowledged the rapturous reception of the audience and walked off the stage, thinking absently that yet another key moment in her musical career had occurred when she wasn't dressed for it.

'You were amazing—'

'Congratulations—'

'A million times better than Callie—'

The praise flowed over her and Izzy pinned a smile on her face, muttered, 'Thank you,' repeatedly as she ploughed her way backstage towards the exit.

She was done. Finished.

'Wait!'

His deep voice froze her limbs and she contemplated making a run for it but as usual her heels were too high to allow a speedy exit so she stood on shaking legs while he caught up with her.

'You sang brilliantly. They love you.'

Izzy heard a dull roar somewhere in the background and realised it was the audience. 'That's good.' She desperately wanted to escape but Matteo planted himself in front of her.

Black jeans suited him, she thought numbly. He looked sensational.

And then she looked at him properly and saw that those sexy eyes were shadowed, tension visible in every angle of his bronzed, handsome face.

'Your goal the night of the engagement was to use me to boost your career so I don't understand why you're leaving.'

Shaking from head to foot, Izzy reminded herself that her goal right now was to get out of here without making a total fool of herself. 'The concert has been the biggest success ever. I hope you raise a ton of money. And now I really have to—'

'If that's all it was—if you were really only using me to boost your career—then you should carry on using me. I was your Goal of the Day. I should be your Goal of Tomorrow too. Being with me will give you the exposure you need.'

Izzy was so close to the edge she was afraid she was going to tip over any moment. 'You've done your bit.' She tried to be flippant but the words emerged as a whisper and she tried desperately to wriggle out of his firm hold.

'Did I suddenly lose my influence and not know about it? Did my recording studio burn down when I wasn't looking?' His tone was savage. 'Was that really all our relationship was to you?'

She'd never seen him like this before and her heart sprinted. 'What was our relationship to you, Matt?'

Her question was greeted by a long tense silence and she sighed.

He was never going to change.

The energy left her. 'I can't do this any more.

The stress is going to give me hardened arteries and very possibly an ulcer, and goodness knows what it will do to you. I'm getting out of your life before you crack under the strain of keeping those barriers up. I wish you everything good.'

'No!' His raw tone shocked her and she took a step backwards.

'Really, you're better off with a woman who isn't interested in emotional involvement and actually that's not me. I'm OK with that up to a point but I'm so afraid of saying the wrong thing now I'm not saying anything at all and I'm not even talking about how hard it is not to say "I love you" at critical moments but when I can't even thank you for a gift because it makes you back off, it's time to rethink the whole thing. It's been great and don't think I'm not grateful for everything you've done for my career—'

'Will you stop talking for a moment!' His voice was hoarse. 'Just how hard is it for you not to say "I love you"?'

Slowly her brain unravelled that less than coherent sentence. 'Quite hard. Well, very hard actually. Why do you think I'm leaving? One of these days it will slip out and I'll give you a nervous breakdown.'

His face lost colour. 'You love me? Not just "like"?'

Oh, what the—? 'Yes, I love you, but seriously *don't* freak because I'm leaving. Right now. Plane is waiting.' She pointed over his shoulder. 'Over there.'

'If you love me, why are you leaving?'

Exasperation bubbled up inside her. 'Apart from everything I've just said? Firstly there's the small fact that you're never going to trust a woman again, and while I don't entirely blame you for that given what happened, I can't live like that. Secondly there's the tiny fact that I am a disaster and five minutes with me will probably ruin all the good work you've ever done. I'm actually being unselfish here and believe me that's not something I do lightly. I'm a very selfish person so just accept the gesture and move out of my way.'

'No.'

Wound tight, Izzy exploded. 'Now *you're* the one being selfish. Eventually you're going to stomp on my heart and I'd rather get it over with now. I'm no good with suspense.'

He gave a ragged laugh and closed his hands over her arms. 'You're right that I'm selfish and there's no way I'm giving you up.'

Izzy glared through her tears. 'I just—'

'Ever.'

The word penetrated her numbed brain. 'Ever?'

'I love you too. You have no idea how much.' The confession was delivered with so much sincerity that she couldn't breathe.

'You're right,' Izzy said faintly, 'I have no idea. Just how much exactly?'

'More than is comfortable.' With a groan, he wrapped his arms around her and held her tightly. 'There is just no way I'm letting you go. From now on my Goal of Every Day is to make you happy.'

Trapped against his chest, Izzy didn't move. He loved her?

Happiness soared like a bird taking its first flight and then plummeted back to earth.

'Even if you do,' she mumbled, 'it's no good.'

'What is no good?' He eased her away from him. 'Don't even think of arguing.'

'I'd ruin everything for you. I'm already ruining things for you. Did you think I didn't see the headlines this morning? *Prince and the Popstar?*' The tears were falling now, brimming up in her eyes and flowing down her cheeks because however hard it had seemed before it was even worse now she knew he loved her. 'They're saying that

I'm using you to further my career. In fact, they're saying a lot worse than that, but never mind—the point is that I'm a tabloid journalist's idea of fast food.'

His eyes gleamed. 'We do a great burger and fries at the palace.'

She turned scarlet at the reminder of her episode with the microphone. 'You see? That's just another example of how I'll embarrass you. I'm a quick, cheap story because no matter what I'm doing I'm probably doing it wrong. Saying the wrong thing, doing the wrong thing—' her voice hitched '—and you don't need that sort of person by your side. You need someone like Katarina whatsername, the perfect society girl you were with before, who is never going to put her elegant foot in anything grimy. My foot is permanently in a cow pat.'

He raised an eyebrow. 'You could try keeping your shoes on.'

'How can you make a joke?' She thumped his chest. 'Let me finish because I have to say this and then I'm going. When I first met you I thought you were cold, arrogant and unfeeling. I thought you were a raging snob, if I'm honest. But then I saw everything that you do and I started to under-

stand. I saw that the reason your reputation matters to you is not because you think you're better
than anyone else, but because you've realised just
how much influence you have and you use that
influence to do good. You took all those vile ex-
periences you had when people only wanted you
because you were a prince and instead of becoming twisted and cynical, you turned it into a positive.'

Matteo muttered something in Italian. 'Izzy,
I *am* cynical. Maybe not twisted, but definitely
cynical. At least, I was until I met you.'

'And then you met me and now you're twisted
too?' Her laugh bordered on the hysterical and he
took her face in his hands and forced her to look
at him.

'I'm not surprised that when you met me you
thought I was a raging snob. I behaved appallingly towards you, and yes, I judged on appear-
ances and every time you sing that song it shames
me because it reminds me of how shallow I was.'

'I was the one who behaved appallingly.' Izzy
groaned. 'And that's what I'm trying to say to
you. No matter how hard I try, I'm always going
to mess up. Even when I make an effort I have a
talent for doing the wrong thing and then think-

ing about it afterwards. It seemed like a perfectly sensible idea to sing at the engagement until I thought about it afterwards. Even swimming in your fountain felt logical—'

'I've discovered that I love swimming in my fountain.'

Tears slid down her cheeks. 'Don't do this. Just…don't. For the first time in my life I'm being unselfish!'

'*Per meraviligia*, don't cry,' he breathed. 'I never want to see you cry. How is it unselfish to walk out on me?'

'Because if we stay together the press coverage won't be good. It won't be all about the good work you do. It will be about my stupid dress sense or other equally irrelevant facts. And people will lose respect for you and then they won't trust you with their money. And you help so many people…' She felt him brush away her tears with his thumb. 'I'm walking away and protecting your reputation.'

'Do you honestly think I'm going to let you do that after what we've shared? You think I'm unselfish but the truth is I've channelled my energies into helping other people to fill the hours of my empty life.' His voice was harsh. 'After what happened I could never allow myself to get close to anyone. I've had plenty of relationships but I've only ever known intimacy with one woman. You. I never thought that could happen. And yes, I've fought against it because frankly it scared the hell out of me. I never thought I would share my life with anyone but then I met you.'

'Me.' Her heart bumped hard. 'Izzy Jackson. A national joke.'

'Izzy Jackson, the bravest, boldest, most hard-working woman I've ever met. I predict that you will soon be a national inspiration and the people of Santina will love you as much as I do.' He brushed the tears from her eyes with a gentle hand and she sniffed.

'You *really* love me?'

'A frightening amount.'

'You can't be more frightened than I am. I—I suppose I'm not used to intimacy either,' she admitted. 'No one in my family is exactly demonstrative.'

'Get used to it.' He lowered his head and kissed her mouth. 'I love the fact that you know what you want and you're not afraid to go for it. I love the fact that you haven't let other people's opinions stop you doing what you want to do. I admire everything about the way you've conducted yourself. No matter what happens you *refuse* to give up.'

Behind them, someone cleared his throat discreetly. 'Your Highness—' one of the concert committee hovered at a safe distance '—you're going to be needed on stage in two minutes. They're expecting you to say a few words.'

'I'll be there when I've finished what I'm doing.' Matteo didn't shift his gaze from Izzy and she tried to push him away.

'They're waiting for you.'

'Let them wait. This is more important.'

'I'm more important than an audience of millions?'

'Right now you're the only audience that matters to me.' He drew in a breath. 'I know you don't have princess aspirations but could I persuade you to change your mind about that?'

Izzy was so shocked she couldn't speak.

'I'm asking you to marry me.' He gave a wry smile. 'Princess Izzy.'

Her legs felt like rubber. She opened her mouth but no sound came out.

'Say something!' His accent was thickened. 'I love you. I want you by my side and together we can do great things or "amazing" things as you would say, as that seems to be your favourite word.'

Still Izzy didn't respond and she heard him curse softly.

'The crowd is waiting. I have to go onto that stage and speak and I want to say it with you standing by my side as my future wife.'

Izzy gulped. 'You want me by your side?' It was just a whisper but apparently it was enough for him.

'Tonight and tomorrow night and the night after that—' his voice was husky '—because that is what people do when they are in love and I am as much in love with you as you are with me. So will you come, Izzy—*bellissima*? I want to introduce the world to my princess.'

In a state of disbelief, Izzy took his hand and they walked back towards the stage.

Happiness bubbled up inside her as it slowly dawned on her that this was real. She lifted her face to look at him. 'I think I'm going to look cute in a tiara. I've never worn anything sparkly on my head before.'

He laughed and tightened his grip on her hand. 'First thing tomorrow I'm going to buy you one.'

'Slow down.' She winced and stooped to fiddle with her feet. 'My shoes are hurting.'

'This is not news. Your shoes are always hurting, *tesoro*.'

'Do princesses absolutely have to wear shoes at all times?'

A slow smile spread across his face and he scooped her into his arms and carried her the last few steps onto the stage. 'Of course not. Didn't you read *Cinderella*?'

* * * * *